Love, Work, and the Other Things

by

John Edward White

TEAMGRUDEN

PUBLISHING

TEAMGRUDEN PUBLISHING

Copyright @2020 by John Edward White

Cover art and design by ©Angela Carole Brown

ISBN: 978-0-578-78934-7

Other books by John Edward White

Dog Lessons - How Raising a Guide Dog Taught Me to See

Hard Reset - a Martin Gardens Novel

A Piece of the Rock - a Martin Gardens Novel

This collection of stories is dedicated to my mother for a lifetime of encouragement and support.

Love, Work, and the Other Things

Table of Contents

Castle Green Parakeet

The parakeet lay curled and stiff along the granite path. A member of the order psittaciformes expired and forgotten, left for the merchants of putrefaction and decomposition to render its hollow boned, skeletal remains to dust. My stomach churned at the indignity and a searing, acrid bile rose in my throat. I stooped to examine the lambent greens and yellow slashes across the primaries, lifted the lifeless body, touched the delicate down of the breast and noted the unusual identification band. This creature was a pet, a cherished and valued companion; someone had lost a loved one and most certainly was grief stricken. Nothing less than dignified interment was required. I wrapped my charge in my sweatshirt, stashed it deep beneath an oleander bower and issued a pungent belch. The males in my family reacted to grief and inconstancy with our stomachs; it is both our legacy and curse. Each learns to listen to his gut, the only true barometer of the heart, and trust its rumblings. Every mistake I'd made in my life could be attributed to ignoring gastronomical red flags. My gut always told me the right thing to do.

I'd been hiking a loop of this wilderness park for nearly five years, logging entries in my journal, accumulating the usual suspects for my life list field record. I knew every square foot of the territory. The thick eucalyptus grove of tall, strong trees with ample, fine branches for nests; the shallows of the dribbling creek ideal for bathing, the gradually sloping foothills of indigenous shrubs and bushes ripe with Spring berries. There were a mating pair of red-tailed hawks I'd been studying the past three seasons that always returned to the same nest constructed high in an ancient fire-blackened pine, and a lone, crippled haggard that appeared infrequently with damaged tarsus and broken primaries on one wing. It settled awkwardly into a crouch wherever it landed, balancing tenuously on its crippled pin, and with its every absence my stomach clenched a little tighter with a kinship we shared. Buteos, like most creatures, need companionship to survive, and this one was alone. Even though I make my living working in a specimen lab testing pathogens, I am quite familiar with all accipitridae; North American raptors are my specialty.

The winter before last, along the bank of the drainage channel, I had sighted a quarrelsome family of burrowing owls, four in number, occupying uninhabited rodent burrows and arguing with each other. I spent an entire afternoon hidden in the underbrush with my Audubon guide to verify field marks and record the sighting in my logbook. I brought Moira here on our third date to show her the diminutive quartet. She perched on a smooth rock, kicked off her sandals and splashed her feet in the water while we waited. We met two years ago at a stadium music festival. It was fate, really. My original seat was a nosebleed aerie almost directly behind the third base foul line pole, but I had hopped from one section to another, each time settling lower in the stands, to gain a better view. She was dancing next to my seat when she twirled and tumbled into my lap. With her freckled face and striking crest of spiky, red hair, she reminded me of the female Vermilion Flycatcher (I had not a single entry in my logbook for the Vermilion Flycatcher, a rarity this far north of the Mexico border). She looked me square in the eye, butted her head against mine, took my hand and led me to a stairway landing crowded with dancers. My stomach fluttered as she pulled me into the group and we began to dance. I am an angular man of below-average height, made mostly of flailing elbows and knobby patellas in awkward motion when I dance, and though Moira was half-a-head taller, she moved with effortless, avian grace. She leaped into the air, flipped her hands out to her sides, and flapped her arms like the red-crested pileated woodpecker, a common North American picidae and the largest woodpecker in America, settling to nest. She began spinning, stopped, stretched her long, pale neck, and without apprehension, fell backward against the crowd. They cheered in unison as they caught her and thrust her back to her feet. This sweet, freckled bill eyass stole my heart. We went to Denny's and talked until almost sunrise. I listened, stared into her washed out blue eyes, and with each word she spoke I fell deeper into love. Not much of a coffee man, I drank cup after cup, heavily laden with milk, and squirmed uneasily on the vinyl bench. My stomach gurgled and my bladder strained to bursting but I wanted to stay close, afraid that if I let her out of my sight, she might abandon our booth. She ordered french fries and added extra salt but not ketchup because it was made from genetically engineered hybrid tomatoes and nibbled each one at a time as she related in a singsong voice growing up with her aunt (her mother died when she was young and she never knew her father), the rhythm of the universe, the collective unconscious of personal spirituality and the holy divinity of all creatures. She never wore makeup because it was tested on animals and brushed her teeth with baking soda and water. She'd quit her job at a pet store because she couldn't stand seeing birds caged or incestuously bred like sex slaves (a common practice among all breeders and not abnormal in the wild), found a job at a used furniture store, and said that her aunt still lived nearby. With each word she uttered I rocked and squirmed, stomach churning in resounding gurgles that migrated south and accidentally escaped in a quavering *pwit*. I sheepishly apologized as she bobbed her head and sniffed the air.

"You don't have to apologize," she said. "All natural creatures do it. As she talked on and on I lost myself in the hypnotic rhythm of her singsong voice and daydreamed about our future together. I imagined a blissful life, a mews high in the hills overlooking the city, the number of our fledglings and their names; as she spoke I was actively sorting out each and every detail of a life together. After breakfast, she took my arm in hers as we walked to a dusty, rufous Tercel and I couldn't stop myself from smiling. The morning sunshine blazed down on us, pressed shoulder to shoulder, like Mother Nature's benediction. My heart pounded, stomach rumbled, and bowels ached to explode. She bent over and placed her ear above my belt to listen and laughed, and then she pecked me on the cheek and sniffed both sides of my neck before she got into her car. I squirmed, stepping forward then backward, jigging side to side and grinning like an idiot. As she drove away I flew straight for the restroom. Perspiration beaded on my forehead and I just made it in time, squatting giddy and giggling at my present good fortune and constitutional relief. I realized I didn't know much about her, but I knew enough to be smitten. I washed my hands, splashed water on my face and fluffed my hair into a victorious spike like the male Vermilion Flycatcher just so I could be her mate.

On the drive home, first I was overcome with pure joy and then I was overcome with pure panic. This was too good to be true; nothing like this happened in real life. I talked myself into and out of and then back into love pacing around my studio apartment, drank half a bottle of loganberry wine and ate an entire sleeve of soda crackers. I vowed to act decisively, throw caution to the wind, and do whatever it took to win Moira over. I took two tablespoons of sodium bicarbonate in warm water and watched Rod Taylor woe Tippi Hedren. Despite all those crazy birds, and their personality differences, somehow they mated.

The next day, on our first real date, everything fell into place. Though we'd only just met, I was convinced that I'd finally found my match. Palpable warmth calmed my dyspeptic stomach. When we were together I felt uncharacteristically bold and spontaneous. I held her hand as we walked and I kissed her beautiful, delicate mouth at the end of the date and she kissed me back. At her front door I sighted a rare Nashville Warbler, normally in Mexico at this time of year, resting in the eaves of her neighbor's house. We were both impressed and she considered it a good omen. The next night she made me dinner in her tiny, garage apartment, and after eating we made passionate love still wearing our socks. This must be what love is, I told her, this fornicating with reckless abandon. Within three weeks we were discussing living together. My stomach glowed with contentment and my bowel rang clear as a bell. We spent every available minute together, discussing our future, imagining the rest of our life together. One month later I found an affordable, second-story apartment with a washing machine in the single-car garage and a claw-foot bathtub. The building was run-down and old but the living room had a picture window overlooking a sloping hill populated by a colony of passerine songbirds and a flock of vivid green, feral parrots nesting in native oaks. In the spirit of bold spontaneity, I recklessly rented the apartment on the spot and spent the afternoon decorating. I tied two yellow balloons to the doorknob, draped a voluminous swag of bright, red ribbon over the doorway and lined up my collection of colorful antique, glass electrical insulators along the sill of the picture window. I brought Moira over that evening, a bouquet of fresh flowers in my hand, and we sat with a bottle of wine and bread on the carpet by the picture window as the moonlight refracted in the glass insulators. This would be our love nest, ours alone, I told her, and she smiled and poked her hand through the moonbeams enveloping us. The next day I moved in my black leather sofa, television, kitchen table and chairs, her kitchen dishes and tall, canopy bed. We had identical, IKEA dressers that I stacked to form a high platform that she covered with a woven hemp dhurrie and miniature Buddha birdbath, and she had a collection of brightly colored scarves that she draped on every available hook and peg. I bought a small bookshelf of unfinished pine for her metaphysical library and my college biology texts. Although I could not wipe the silly lovesick grin from my face, occasionally my stomach rumbled with anxiety and the relentless foreboding that something this good only happened in the movies.

When I returned to the apartment, Moira was standing on one foot (just like the Great Egret found on all continents and almost hunted to extinction in the 20th century for its magnificent veil of white plumes), balancing in the doorway, an umbrella stand on her crooked knee as she locked the door, looked at my rolled sweatshirt and sniffed.

"What's that," she asked.

"A parakeet."

"Smells like leaves."

"I think that's me," I said and we laughed.

"I'll be back later," she said.

"Where're you going?"

"Work. First I have to stop by Auntie's," she said as she floated off, the striking crest of spiky, red hair disappearing down the stairway. We'd been through this before; she would take a piece of furniture from the apartment whenever she went to visit her aunt. One week there would be a coat rack by the door; a week later that would be replaced with an umbrella stand. A dictionary trestle, which I was going to use for my oversized, illustrated Audubon bird book, came and went overnight. I think I remember some kind of wood, garden bench, too. She was incessantly remodeling our love nest. The only pieces never liberated were those in the bedroom, my kitchen table and chairs, and the black leather sofa that I knew required at least two people to move. When I complained that I couldn't get used to furniture coming and going, she'd say, "Less is more. Natural creatures don't confuse wants with needs." If I questioned her behavior, she would grow silent, bob around the apartment, pluck things off the kitchen table or the black leather sofa and toss them onto the floor. Then she would sit at the edge of the picture window scanning the empty sky and refuse to talk. She'd sulk until I said I was sorry and then fantastic make-up sex would follow. We'd roll around on the carpet, shedding clothes, circling each other on all fours and butting heads in a mixture of dominant aggression and sexual passion. Her pale skin would flush all over and a triangular birthmark near the base of her spine would glow bright red. She'd call out in that singsong voice 'we're breeding' and leap to her feet dancing from room to room, tugging scarves from where they hung and banding them in colorful patches around her neck, her wrists and ankles, or wrapped around her forehead like a veil in front of her washed out, blue eyes. Finally, she'd let me pin her in the front room and while we mated she'd quietly cack and then at climax cheep repeatedly, just like the secret and solitary Sprague's Pipit's flight song, reminiscent of the Old World Skylark and sung in melodious two-note phrases as it ascends out of sight. (Sadly, the mellifluous Pipits with their large dark eyes are much reduced in range and numbers across the Prairie Provinces along the Canadian border.) Then we'd lie side by side in a blanket staring out the picture window, her pale skin against mine, moonbeams refracting around the glass insulators on the sill, and talk about starting a brood of our own. When we grew cold, I'd fill the claw-foot bathtub and we'd sit with our legs entwined below the bubbles and groom each other's back in post-coital afterglow. We'd dry off and cling together in the tall, canopy bed and I'd fall asleep to a calm stomach. She was like some sort of divine compensation for my many lonely days and nights and it scared me how perfect it felt.

I tossed my sweatshirt and some clothes into the washer and placed the parakeet on the lid. As the machine filled and agitated, the bird rolled from side to side with the vibration. Its still wings splayed limply and I think I saw the body twitch. I took off my hiking boots and stood to examine the fallen aviator. I couldn't help but feel a hint of sadness. Every order of birds lives a life far too short. This parakeet lived a life and like all living things that life had come to a lonely end. No mate chirping compassionately from a nearby perch; no offspring gathering at the bower to bear witness to a fruitful existence. It perished frighteningly, absolutely, alone. I remembered exactly that very feeling: a constant, unremitting ache in the pit of my stomach like nature's insistent admonishment against solitude, and thought about the solitary haggard with the crippled tarsus at the wilderness park. I could imagine his unjust destiny in the fallen parakeet as I held the carcass in my palms and felt the fragility of its body. The beak was clean, the body plump and feathers well groomed. Soft and for some reason still warm, it was a complete creature with everything necessary to sustain life but life itself. My stomach began to churn furiously and a fiery iron poker prodded my bowels. I felt hot, clammy and flushed as I shuffled upstairs to the toilet and experienced an unpleasant onslaught of cramps and loose stools. After some minutes, my face cooled and the cramps subsided. I felt better, went to the kitchen and drank half a bottle of magnesium in suspension. I retrieved the parakeet, sat at the kitchen table, and examined the irregular identification band bent awkwardly around the ankle. I carefully prised it apart, unrolling it with a butter knife and a pair of kitchen drawer pliers. On one side of the crudely cut band was a segment of the Pepsi logo; on the other side, scratched in the bare aluminum, was a telephone number with a local area code. The first call rang and rang. I waited a few minutes and called again. The phone was answered on the second ring. A woman's voice, augmented by rustling in the background, chirped from the receiver.

"What for?" she said when I explained that I had her parakeet.

"I found it alongside a hiking path," I said.

"Why are there so many paths?"

"She's deceased, Maam," I replied.

"Desdemona belong to Castle Green," she said and I swear I heard the unmistakable trill of the common house wren in the background.

"But she's dead," I said.

"No No No! Desdemona here," she squawked. "With mate!"

"I'm terribly sorry, about this. I'm an amateur ornithologist myself, a birder, actually, although my specialty is raptors, so I understand."

"Bring," she commanded and then screeched, "I am safe keeper. Hurry! Bring now!" The line went dead. I sat for a moment and looked around the nearly empty apartment. It was almost one-o'clock and Moira wouldn't be home from work until after five. My stomach idled comfortably with the creamy metallic coating of antacid and my brow was dry to the touch. I bound Desdemona in an organic, lavender scarf, placed her in a shoebox, pulled on tee shirt and jacket and closed the door on my way out.

I recognized the name at once. My uncle Marion, a stalwart man, remembered for his tremendous head of red hair, predatory libido and a collection of carved, ivory-headed walking canes of which he was quite proud, lived at the Castle Green. When I visited him before he died, on my seventh birthday, he confided to my confused countenance that he resided at the Castle Green because it not only came with room and board but, and he winked a pale blue eye, "my favorite cousin, if you know what I mean."

The Castle Green was five stories, with Moorish-influenced window treatments and sheltered stone ledges perfect for perches and nests. Each suite had a gas fireplace, and some suites were interconnected. Through the years, the Castle had slipped into a state of general decrepitude, appealing mostly to romantic eccentrics willing to tolerate the absence of modern conveniences. People could rent apartments by the month and many did. Although it was run down, you could still see its remnants of majesty and grandeur.

I walked along the top floor past Marion's old room. The brass number plate I remembered was gone. Two dark holes and a faint rectangular outline remained on his door. I proceeded to the next apartment and knocked. I knocked again, set the shoebox against the door, turned to leave and then picked it up again. This was one of nature's finest creations; at the very least it deserved more than to be abandoned in a hallway. I knocked once more, with greater vigor, and instantly the pinched face of a petite, hoary woman wearing a battered straw hat appeared in the doorway. She thrust her head out and held the door close about her neck. Flashes of light and shadow shot behind her, accompanied by pronounced rustling. A saline odor like marsh brine wafted through the doorway. Above her battered straw hat, birds passed one after another, from near to distant, as far as I could see into the room. There must have been hundreds. I stared in disbelief and she tilted her hooked nose upward and smiled gleaming, strong white teeth. Birds flashed past and though I know it to be impossible, I swear that I sighted a pair of east coast Blue Jays, abnormal anywhere in the western region, especially at this time of year. I could not believe my eyes. The door slammed shut and within seconds Uncle Marion's old door swung open and the tiny woman emerged in a stained, yellow rain slicker, knee high rubber boots and sou'wester. She sprang through the door and pulled it closed behind her. With mincing steps she hurried down the hallway, bobbing side to side, turned and tilted her hooked nose invitingly in my direction. I shifted my package from hand-to-hand, aware of the slightest movement within the shoebox. At the end of the hallway, she stopped at a pair of French doors and lifted the brim of her sou'wester to reveal her eyes.

"Ornithologist," she sneered through dry, cracked lips and began bouncing up and down and joyously flapping her arms. Then she stepped through the French doors onto a small, railed balcony and with remarkable dexterity thrust her leg over the railing and reached in a sort of falling motion toward a fixed, iron-rung ladder. She was already up and climbing onto the roof while I was contemplating the five-story exposure and corroded iron rungs. She stood on the rooftop, peered at me with only her prominent beak visible beneath the sou'wester, and flapped her arms in mockery. I took Desdemona from the shoebox, tucked her into my jacket and followed.

The entire west end of the building was an exposed assembly of rusted pipes. On every section perched fat dusty pigeons, cooing mourning doves, mottled wrens, Brewers sparrows, shore gulls of all species, Stellar jays, scrub jays, mockingbirds, more vivid green parrots, a yellow parakeet, and a swarming charm of house finches. Above us, socially oversensitive crows circled and cawed. The roof was thick with scat, and a continuous stream fell as various birds arrived and departed. The old woman, sou'wester tied beneath her chin, stood at a valve above a narrow, copper trough. She opened the valve, water flowed and birds dived and fluttered, swooping and landing and skimming along the rim. It was like a scene from the Hitchcock movie, as hundreds of birds filled the sky angling for a perch at the copper trough. She waited until it was nearly full, shut off the valve and crossed the roof in her mincing gait. She went straight to the ladder without hesitation and disappeared. I followed her cautiously, taking my time climbing down and transitioning to the railed balcony, and stopped before the door to her apartment. As I stood in the hallway, the unmistakable presence of activity within my jacket could not be ignored.

A weak, crack of diffused light emitted as the door opened. I peered into the dim interior and the old woman motioned me inside. She had discarded the raincoat for a plaid bathrobe and replaced the sou'wester with the battered straw hat. As my eyes adjusted to the darkness, shapes floated in front and behind. The room was bare of furniture, but assembled from floor to ceiling was a white, geodesic structure of white, plastic, irrigation pipe. It formed multiple levels of tees, right angle joints and long, horizontal sections. On each section pigeons, doves, feral parrots and oscine songbirds perched. The colony sang at ear-splitting volume in a raucous chorus. More birds whooshed in and out wide, casement windows. A solitary, yellow parakeet swooped in and out of view. In the center of the room was a half-filled children's wading pool. In it was an overturned wheelbarrow, missing the wheel, with half a dozen birds shuffling along the axle. They dropped to the water, splashed and returned to fluff and preen. It was fantastic. The petite woman stood to one side, birds on her shoulders, her straw hat and more clinging to her back. She bowed toward me, picked up an ivory-headed cane and danced from one side of the room to the other, the birds riding comfortably on her person, as she swept the cane beneath the pipes. The birds rose and settled. She lifted her arms skyward, grabbed the cane with both hands, thrust her hips from side to side, spun slowly on her heels and once more swept the cane beneath the birds. I looked for a place to set Desdemona. On one side of the entrance a wood, garden bench had been laid upside down across the pipes to form perches and a shelf. As respectfully as I could, I unwrapped my charge. There, directly beneath the bench, wrapped in a plastic shower curtain, I recognized the umbrella stand. A very familiar coat rack, encrusted in ropy scat and fully occupied, stood near the casement windows. Our dictionary trestle lay on its side in the corner of the room. The old woman approached, picked up Desdemona and placed her on the overturned wheelbarrow. She spread the wings, sprinkled water from the pool onto Desdemona's head, clapped her hands and began to whirl about the room chanting in a singsong voice that excited the birds as the cane swung wildly and bounced off the plastic pipes sending pigeons and doves into flight. The woman continued her gyrations, the birds rising and hovering each time she passed her cane beneath them. She spun and spun, whipping more and more birds into the air, waving the cane

19

over Desdemona's lifeless body. The bird's raucous chorus was deafening. I covered my ears with both hands and retreated to the safety of the doorframe. The entire room was filled with birds, darting and diving, fluttering, landing and darting again as more and more came gliding through the open windows. The birds perched on her shoulders, straw hat and back, cloaking her in chattering cries and flapping wings. Her entire body was covered. She continued spinning, waving the cane over Desdemona again and again, and more and more birds circled in motion with her. I groped behind me for the doorknob, unable to take my eyes from the frenzied montage. All at once, the old woman stopped, threw her arms out to her sides and fell backward. An army of birds dove beneath her and frantically fanned the air. She hung suspended at an acute angle, supported by the multitude of birds. More birds joined the others at her back. Slowly, she righted, extending her arms forward with her hands pressed together in obeisance, and bowed. The birds exploded in every direction, shrieking and tearing around the room in a chaotic celebration of molting feathers and flapping wings. I was awestruck at the spectacle and exiting, I swear, I saw Desdemona standing upright on the wheelbarrow beside the yellow parakeet.

Back at our apartment, I told Moira about the bird woman of Castle Green and my Uncle Marion. I didn't comprehend the inevitable logic of the words until it was too late to unsay them. Moira got a horrified look on her face and covered her ears. I reached for her as tears ran down her cheeks. She pushed me away and covered her beautiful, delicate mouth with her hand. "That means you're my, my…" she sputtered. She plucked at her crown of red hair and stomped her feet. "It isn't fair," she shouted. "I love you, too." I tried to catch her, but she darted out of reach and flew out the door, unresponsive to my earnest pleading. I sat down to reason it out and waited. I told myself to remain calm; this was something we could work through, a common occurrence in the natural world and one which every breeder confronts in selecting the more promising candidates for a species' propagation. I telephoned Moira's only girlfriend, but she wouldn't talk to me. I paced until almost dawn, my stomach churning and finally fell asleep on the floor beneath the picture window. The next day I called the apartment from the lab and the phone rang and rang. I left early and when I got home all her things were gone. The dresser draws were open and empty, her clothes removed from the closet, the library of metaphysical books absent from the bookshelf. I was heart broken. I looked everywhere, spent the week searching, tried everyone she might know, drove myself to exhaustion in my attempt to track her. I couldn't sleep or eat. My stomach turned permanently sour and I subsisted on sodium bicarbonate, magnesium in solution, and frozen pizza. Over and over again I returned to the bird woman's apartment but no one answered my knock. On my final visit I located the landlord. He told me that the apartment had been vacated with no forwarding address, and the bird lady had left with a young woman with red hair. Though I tried everything I could to find her, I never heard from Moira again. That was two years ago and sometimes I still have trouble sleeping. I gave up drinking coffee, developed an intolerance for wine shortly after her disappearance, and to this day find french fries indigestible. Outside my picture window, the sloping hill has been razed, the passerine songbirds have scattered, feral parrots evicted, and a family home is under construction. During the day, men wearing tool belts and hard hats cut lumber and pound nails. In place of indigenous foliage and the volunteer stand of native oaks, a human nest is erected stick by stick. I can see the framework and imagine what a fine home it might be if it were roofless and high in the tops of the uprooted trees, nothing between it and the stars but endless miles of soaring, clear blue sky. I think about Moira, sitting at night near the picture window, and wonder where she might be. I live with a constant dull ache in the pit of my stomach that flares and settles but never disappears, and when I get home from the lab I check my phone machine as soon as I enter the apartment, wishing against all logic that her voice will be waiting. When I think back on it, the whole thing was like a dream; it was too good to be true. Life isn't like a movie.

The Truth About Men

It was nothing more than pure coincidence, being there at that exact moment, standing at the kitchen sink of his second story unit and looking down across the alley into her bedroom window. She entered and removed her blouse and sloughed her brassiere onto the bed. She loosened her skirt, wiggled it from her hips, folded it on the bed, tugged at her waist, sat, stood, and swept hose and panties toward the corner of the room. All at once she was nothing more than sculpted rises and rounds, pale contiguous curves immaculate and beautiful. She pulled a purple kimono from the bedroom door and disappeared from view. The entire disrobing required no more than thirty seconds and it took his breath away.

She drove a white, rust-mottled Toyota and parked beneath a denuded jacaranda at the rear of the complex. There was no mistaking the identity of the vehicle: the rattle of the disemboweled muffler, the rough idle as the motor stumbled and coughed. The driver's door would swing open and a battered black pump would hunt for purchase on the chunked asphalt. There were always groceries to be unloaded or baskets of laundry to be carried inside. Except alternate weekends, she would be accompanied by a dark-haired boy. He would race, with his backpack and sports equipment, around the corner and out of sight. She wore the same pair of battered, black pumps almost every day except when she wore knee-high leather boots and tight, black jeans. He especially liked her in the jeans.

*   *   *

Each time was just like the first, except now she wore the battered black pumps and spent a few minutes stretching her arms over her head, flexing her hips from side to side as she fluffed her dark hair with one hand and caressed her breasts with the other. After that, she'd reach for the kimono, kick free the battered black pumps and switch off the overhead light. One time, she stepped close to the window and looked toward his apartment with a thin smile on her mouth, as if she were silently amused, before she rounded the corner out of sight. He watched her performance from his kitchen for a whole week.

*   *   *

Friday, he perched on his tall stool at the design table and waited for his cube mate to settle into his chair.

"I think I've done something wrong," he said. "I've been watching the woman next door."

His cube mate, a bear-like man in his late fifties with tremendous mustaches that drooped beneath his nose and draped past his chin, put one leg over the other and squeezed his brown eyes into slits. His baldhead was a rectangular block, the greater length extending front to rear, a barely perceptible crevice stepped midway from ear to ear. His brow was plowed with a single furrow terminating at his temples and his face was perfectly flat. His nose was no more than a suggestion, the nostrils askew at slightly conflicting vertical and horizontal attitudes. He snapped his head to one side with an audible crunch, raised a can of Dr. Pepper high over his head and drained a stream of dark, sparkling syrup into his mouth.

"Watching?"

"Peeping, I suppose, is more accurate."

"I see."

He crossed his thick forearms over his thick thighs and looked up from beneath thick, bushy eyebrows.

"I didn't begin to peep, you know. It just happened."

The cube mate used his toe to open a desk drawer and eased his boot heel into the recess. He looked at his watch and smoothed his mustaches with thumb and forefinger.

"Whom, if I may so inquire, is it that you have 'Peeped'?"

"My neighbor, next door, in the ground level apartment."

"I see."

The cube mate fingered the empty soda can, placed it on the desk blotter and very slowly compressed it beneath a beefy palm. The man sat up straight and squared his shoulders and peered into his cube mate's face.

"I've seen her undressing," he said. "I've seen her more than once."

*   *   *

He was washing his car late Saturday afternoon when the Toyota entered his drive. She drove absently, staring straight ahead and stopped, the motor stumbling and coughing as it struggled to idle. She sat motionless, cheeks streaked with dark mascara, eyes filled and spilling. The hose dribbled at his feet, a dripping oval sponge held in one hand as he stared at her across the hood of his car. Panic crossed her face, her almond shaped eyes found his and shifted with recognition. She twisted her head, ground the transmission into reverse and frantically backed out of view. He heard the tires scrub on the pavement, the motor race and the brakes squeal, and then the car shot down the driveway next door. Before he could speak, she exited head bowed and slope-shouldered with her hands making a church covering nose and mouth. He watched as she disappeared into her apartment, sentences in his mind still forming, arrested somewhere between thought and speech. As he put away the sponge, bucket and hose he reviewed his speech, refining each sentence, imagining how he would walk to her door, how she would open it, how she would respond when he spoke. Dusk came and he moved his car to his assigned parking space. He sat and watched lights appear in windows of the apartments next to hers. Overhead, the jetliners howled as they lowered their landing gear on approach to LAX with blinking green and red wing lights defining their route. He listened for some time, counting the jets, went upstairs when he reached 13 and peered at her dark bedroom window.

It wasn't until noon of the next day that he saw her. She was dressed in a pleated, gray and burgundy plaid skirt and a plain white blouse. She carried a blue cardigan sweater over one arm, a bible, and a small black handbag over her shoulder. She put the sweater, bible, and purse in the passenger seat and climbed into her car. He heard the engine turn over and stop. There was a pause. He heard the starter hammer and then a longer pause. He started for his front door, raced down the stairs determined this time to make her acquaintance as the engine caught. He watched as she drove out of the alley with the engine stumbling and the exhaust note reverberating off the concrete driveway wall. He returned to his kitchen window and watched what he could see until the car disappeared from view.

*   *   *

"What I like best about her is the way she treats her son," he said. "She cups the back of his head with her hand when they walk from the car to her apartment, and I've never heard her scold him."

The cube mate was drinking an enormous, red and green plastic tankard of coffee, the words "Thirsty Thirty-Two Ouncer" emblazoned along the rim. He held it by the handle with a thumb and two fingers and blew across the top. He wore a crisp, tartan plaid dress shirt, the short sleeves reaching beyond his elbows, folds of material billowing across his expansive stomach. He turned from his coffee with a week's worth of beard on his chin and cheeks and a bright, red line of freshly shaved skin along the edge of his throat.

"Huh?"

"I mean, she treats him the way I would treat him. If he were ours."

The cube mate looked to his coffee, drank again and cleared his throat. He rotated in his chair, rocked backwards and found the desk drawer with his heel.

"Maybe you ought to meet and learn a little about the woman before you assume her family."

"But I've got a feeling that this is the right woman for me. I like everything about her: I like the way she dresses, the way she treats her son, the fact that she's religious - I saw her going to church, you know - I admit that I don't really know her, but what is there to that, anyway? If one person is attracted to another person, don't they sort of fill in the parts they don't know? No one's perfect. But I like her looks, her body: I've seen it. I like everything about her."

His cube mate rested his arms on top of his stomach, raised one eyebrow and squinted one eye.

"What, God forbid, if she doesn't like you?"

He sat up slowly.

"You're joking," he said with surprise. "Why wouldn't she like me?"

In the background, keyboards clicked and people moved up and down the aisle. The low frequency drone of air conditioning floated along the acoustic-tile ceiling. A series of frantic mouse clicks was arrested with a series of vulgar expletives. A cabinet drawer slammed closed. The cube mate drained his coffee and balanced the tankard on his knee.

"You still peeping?"

"Not really. I only watch to make sure she's okay, not sick or anything. In case she needs help."

"What would make you think she needs help?"

"I know that she needs help. I can help her."

"Help her how?"

"You know, make her life better."

"I see."

The cube mate rose from his chair, took a section of newspaper from the top of his desk and folded it under his arm. He turned as he stepped into the aisle.

"She must know by now that you're watching."

"How would she know?"

"Women know things."

"They do?"

"Yep."

*   *   *

The next day the man left for a company sponsored Human Factors seminar in Phoenix. He spent an uneventful

30

three days filled with conferences and presentations, and he spent his nights watching television in the hotel. On Thursday night, he boarded a half-empty flight for Ontario Airport. He looked at the in-flight magazine and laid his head back. 'Tomorrow's Friday,' he thought. 'Casual Friday. I wonder if she'll be wearing those jeans?' He sat back and clipped his seat belt into place. 'And it's the end of the month so at least I'll get paid. I'll have some money to take her out so I might as well do it. Now's the time.' A smile crossed his face and the woman seated in his row raised the armrest alongside the vacant seat between them.

"Hello," she said. "I like it when there's a little more room."

"Yes. Me, too."

The plane taxied to the runway, gathered speed and his spine pressed against the back of the seat. They lifted off and he heard the landing gear whir as it retracted and locked into place. Immediately, the plane banked sharply to the left and the woman rolled toward him. Her shoulder pressed tightly to his and as he gripped his armrest and steadied himself he felt her tense. She had one arm across the empty seat between them and he realized that she had grabbed his hand and folded her ringless fingers into his. The plane leveled off and she sighed and without removing her hand turned her face to his.

"I get a little nervous at that part," she said. "I hope you don't mind."

She righted herself and sat back against her seat. Together they looked at their interlocked fingers. The man raised his eyes without removing his hand and studied her face. Her nose was straight and narrow; the end was delicately cleaved. Behind a pair of oversized, tortoise frame, eyeglasses her eyes were bright and blue. The right eye was flecked with a tiny trapezoidal discoloration at the edge of iris. Above their heads the seat belt icon flashed and over the loudspeaker a flight attendant spoke. He began to feel faint and took several deep breaths. She was speaking to him. He forced himself to concentrate on her words but all he could hear was his pounding heart. She removed her eyeglasses and wiped at her eyes with an embroidered linen handkerchief edged in yellow and blue bearing the initials SAM.

"That's okay, really," she said as she placed her eyeglasses in her jacket pocket. "If you don't want to talk, I mean."

He reached above his head for the call light and the air nozzle.

"I'm sorry. I guess I didn't hear you."

She turned in her seat to fix her bright, blue eyes on him.

"Are you all right? You look pale. Here, let me," she said and reached up with her handkerchief and dabbed at his forehead. The flight attendant stopped at their seat row and toggled the call light.

She spoke before he could. "Excuse us. Could we get some water and a damp towel, please?"

"Of course. Is everything all right?"

"We'll be all right."

He studied her face. Beyond her, through the cabin window, gray and white clouds washed past. He sat back and closed his eyes. She took the towel from the flight attendant, put it across his forehead and held it. He reached up for the towel and she helped him, holding the towel with her hand and keeping it positioned over his brow. She handed him the plastic cup of water and he sipped at it and then she took it from him. His breathing evened and he could feel his heartbeat slow. He closed his eyes and began to relax. He awoke with a jerk.

"Easy, I'm right here," she said.

He rubbed at his eyes and looked around the plane.

"You'll be all right; you're looking better already. Maybe something to eat is what you need. When was the last time you ate?"

"Last night, I think; well, not dinner really. Just a snack. I had lunch yesterday at the hotel."

"And nothing all of today? That could explain it."

The pilot announced their approach. He adjusted his seat and fastened the seat belt. Next to him his companion followed suit and the two sat silently as the plane began to descend. He held the damp towel in his hands and thought about the girl at his apartment until the plane touched down. When he looked at his companion she was clenching her jaw.

"We're here, safe and sound," he said.

"Yes."

The plane taxied towards the gate and the passengers shifted in their seats.

"I've never had that happen before. I felt like I was going to pass out."

"You'll be fine," she said. "You just need someone to look after you a little; to remind you to eat," she said and laughed.

The man stood and reached down her bags from the overhead compartment. People were sorting their belongings and beginning to advance on the exit. He stepped back in the aisle to allow her to pass.

"Thank you."

They shuffled along behind the other passengers until they had descended the stairway to the tarmac. The group began to spread out as people strode ahead or stopped to adjust their luggage, some extending handles from their bags while others shifted their briefcases from one shoulder to the other. He stayed beside her until they reached the terminal. She turned to him and set down her bags.

"I'm on my way," she said and smiled. "These are all my bags."

She studied him, one hand on her mouth, bright, blue eyes shining behind the tortoise frame eyeglasses.

"Guess I'll be going," she said.

"Thank you, again. Really. You're very kind."

Her bright, blue eyes momentarily blazed.

"Yes, I truly am."

She looked at him and he dropped his eyes. She paused, shuffled her feet, let out a sigh and picked up her bags.

"Well then. Good bye," she called.

*   *   *

On the drive from the airport he fidgeted with the radio, grew impatient in traffic and began to feel faint. He breathed deeply and thought about his neighbor, her battered Toyota, and planned what he would do first. The car needed a tune-up, probably an oil change as well, and of course some repair on the muffler. He knew he could take care of that. He pulled into his apartment complex and noticed her windows were dark. He climbed the stairs to his apartment, slung his luggage on his bed and began to hang up his clothes and separate his laundry. It was unusual for her courtyard to be vacant of cars. He stopped what he was doing, dropped his

35

laundry basket and ran down the stairs and outside. In the alley next door, a large dumpster was pushed against the garages. His heart pounding, he rounded the corner and ran along the sidewalk of the apartments. Her door was open and except for a mound of tattered sheet rock and carpet remnants, it was empty. The walls were patched in places, the hardwood floors bare, and in the hallway a piece of flooring had been replaced. Each room was in stages of preparation for painting. The stove stood in the center of the front room and in the kitchen cabinets gaped open as if interrupted mid-speech. Along the kitchen windowsill was a single votive candle and book of matches. He closed the front door behind him, returned to his courtyard and went upstairs. Across the alley, barely visible in the darkness, a pair of battered black pumps perched on the edge of her bedroom window. Overhead, he counted the jetliners as they lowered their landing gear and howled on approach. He listened until he lost count, staring at the empty apartment before finally going to bed. It was a long time before he could fall asleep.

Epistemology of Loneliness

Through the early morning fog to the north you can see the narrowing of the valley; a truncated vista collapsing upon itself. To the west are the small holdings of local ranchers and farmers; to the east the great Ethans' ranch. Ethans run Gelbviehs; no Herefords or Holsteins for them: Nothing but show stock, top line beef and some quarter horses. Ethans owned a good part of this land. Kept the best and sold the remainder in small parcels. They mark their property with white, square-rail fences that run for miles. The small rancher's fences are made from rough lumber, leaning precariously toward the highway, the barb wire strands slack or broken. There, standing by the road, is my heron. He is alone, in the same spot as yesterday, watching traffic and bearing a troubled contour on his long slender neck. He looks as though he's waiting for something to happen. I watch him as I pass; look hard into the sadness of his eyes. He follows my truck with his head, the neck arching in a double curve. I think that he is a bit melancholy. I think that he's lost his way; he needs someone. Along the highway is no place for a heron.

Janelle and I split sheets. We've gone separate ways. It was abrupt, no overt warning, just the subterranean vibrations of parting. I felt them in my feet, right through the sidewalk. Two weeks ago I stopped at her store. She was out front, turning the lock and talking with a man. I stood behind a van to watch. The two of them turned and she put her arm in his as they walked. She nuzzled tight to his shoulder, swinging her hips loosely as if she hadn't a care in the world. I stalked them to his Volvo. I could've laid him out then, right there, dropped him to his knees as easy as a sneeze, inflicted monstrous pain and suffering upon his person. I wished it: yuppy asshole. I lit a cigarette and, while they drove away, leaned on a parking meter for support. I felt terrible. I felt the ground move, the meter sway, my stomach collapse with my heart. I smoked another cigarette and then another and heavily I dragged myself to my truck. I wanted to break something, anything, strike quick with ferocious fatality; I felt so beat I could hardly drive. I cursed first her, then him, and then me. It shouldn't have come as a surprise. She draws men like flies. All that blond hair and a figure that she wears like a weapon. At home I opened beer and sat in front of the television. I smoked, drank, mumbled invectives through my stupor, and crawled unbathed into bed. Goddamn her.

The weather is inclement; the visibility is worsening. I slow and turn west on a potted, county road. Set back a few feet from the road are small lots with disintegrating homes. Each has two or more dogs, collapsing outbuildings of peeling paint and rotting timber, and side yards of discarded, partially disassembled automobiles. There is little variance between the properties. Many houses bear the results of improvised improvements: a repaired stoop, multi-colored porch rails, mottled siding of lap strake and plywood; a patchwork of scavenged sheet metal affixed in irregular patterns to roofs, over entrances, filling gaps in lean-to walls. The doomed results of valiant effort are made the more prominent by the disregard of others. The quarters of the abjectly poor. I pass Crane Mills. In the lot are half-a-dozen pick-up trucks, one wrecked semi tractor, two men in cowboy hats leaning against the warehouse. The mill runs about half time; most of the people in the area worked there. With little work, they're forced to sell their homes and their land, leaving ranches that were homesteaded by great-great-grandparents. Some still run cattle; some have sheep. There are no crops here; a few struggling truck gardens and sparse flower beds. The soil is too much clay and rock. It dries like cement in the summer and, in the winter, the rains saturate the ground in minutes, swelling the creeks and washing the garbage from the backyards and side lots. Every few years it will snow and blanket the detritus with a veneer of momentary purity: A futile transmogrification of inevitable decay.

My crew is waiting in front of the Mormon church. Three guys, not much younger than I am, lean against the brick pillars of the refectory entrance. Beyond is the chapel, a formidable structure, three stories of cut granite and red brick with a slate tile roof. The chapel is all you could expect of the house of Joseph Smith. It's imperious, inspirational and commanding. No cost was spared. The uppermost level is framed with stained glass windows, a scene of Mormon significance in colored glass filling each pane. The grounds are stately, painstakingly landscaped with sheltered beds of azaleas, cape weed ground cover, and fruit trees on every side. The lawn was beautiful until we arrived. When we do a sprinkler installation, the trenching and excavating tear up the yard. It shocks the owners, though we try to be as neat as possible, to see their yards laid open with intersecting trenches and mounds of rock and soil. I must admit we could have been much neater. The guys took a special interest in destroying the Mormon's landscape.

It's the most complicated system that I've designed: thirty-six station clock, four programs, a dozen start times, and more than four hundred feet of pipe. The Mormons already had a sprinkler system, but they weren't satisfied. It seems that where you stood when you turned on the valves, you got wet. We could have converted their system fairly easily, replaced the manuals with automatics and tied it to one clock. It would have performed perfectly; they didn't want that. "Replace the whole thing," Clark said; "Make it trouble-free." I didn't argue. It's their money.

The head man, that's Clark, arrives in a blue, late model Buick.

"Hello, I'm Clark Brent."

We've met before.

"How is the work coming? Will it be finished by Saturday? We have a special program planned. I expect a good turnout. The food usually packs them in."

Clark never waits for me to answer. He keeps talking, breathlessly, opening and closing his eyes like trying to clear something from the pupils. I walk him through the site, explaining what's being done and how. He doesn't show much interest. I assure him the grounds will be neat, the dirt moved and the lawn repaired by COB Friday. He makes a hasty exit. One of my guys, Mark, points to a bumper sticker on the rear of Clark's Buick. `Get Right or Get Left.'

The church is still a mess. I spent yesterday stuffing conduit under the roof eaves and felt no closer to god but no farther, either. I'll be on the roof most of today. From the moment I submitted my bid I knew the Mormons were pure hell. They hung me up ten days on the initial installment. The check had to come through Salt Lake, be twice signed, notated and then blessed. My god. The larger the client, the more difficult it is to extract payment. Had to ask my guys to hold their paychecks until I could transfer funds. Couldn't pay the subcontractor who cut the asphalt. Couldn't pay my line man pulling trenches. Small-time entrepreneur, right; small-time one-step from bankruptcy is more like it. I fouled up this job; bid it for thirteen days, and if no more snags develop, it'll run two extra. I should get out with something. That is providing the good Mormons come through.

I set the guys to task. I put Mark back filling trenches, Terry wiring the valves and take Kevin with me to the roof. We get most of the conduit up before lunch, and when we return from eating we purge the system for dirt. Kevin and Terry can put on filters and set heads while I program the clock. By five we're in pretty good shape; maybe two good days and we'll be out of here. Clark is supposed to meet me Thursday to okay the installation. God and good weather providing, he'll bring the check.

I'm an independent contractor. Contractors survive from one job to the next, never knowing when the weather will close you out or renegade luck will prevent you from working. If the work's there, I have to take it. In the between times I have to sell the next one, to keep the crew working, and the cash flowing. I've got payments to make and notes to meet; banks don't offer much latitude on business loans. It's sink or swim, either way, they only want their money. I've managed to stay just ahead of them this season. The Mormon account could really help me out. Maybe get a good referral, too. Have to hustle, that's the way of it. Early bird gets to heaven, late bird gets chapter 11. The way of the world.

After work we stop in front of The Duke and drink a beer in the parking lot. Mark mentions an important date he has with a woman he met in school. We wish him luck with thumbs up and smiles. He acts a bit sheepish and reserved. I take the long way home and pick up material in town. Tomorrow's another day.

*   *   *

In the morning I stop for coffee and a roll, and talk to Maria, the young, crippled girl behind the counter. She must have had polio. She hasn't much movement with one arm, and half steps, half drags one leg when she moves. She's friendly and always remembers my name. `I thought I was blue when I had no shoes, until I met a man who had no feet.' What kind of a country is this that can let something like that happen to a girl. Aren't there required inoculations and boosters for that kind of thing. Christ almighty.

Maria has very long, red hair. She wears it in her cap, but I've seen her with it down before. She's probably eighteen or nineteen, working at a lousy donut hole when she should be in the prime of her life. What kind of social life could she have? She can't dance, or at least not well; probably doesn't get many dates. A doubtful sex life. Maybe I should take her out, do a night on the town. She's no fool, she'd see right through me, I'm sure of it. Some old guy feeling pity and looking to score. I don't want to make her life more miserable.

I notice the smaller the town the more of the handicapped you see. In the big city, I don't know where they go. It's all beautiful people with white teeth and perfect hair. We do jobs in various little towns up and down the valley. In every one you see handicapped; some are mentally retarded, crippled, some disfigured or maimed in a horrible way. What's life have in store for them? What kind of god let's this go on? What mercy and grace is this? I think I'll hurl a few well-chosen remarks from the roof of the church. Should make me feel better.

I do feel better when I get out on the highway. The ranches slide past, Herefords and Angus and a lone Galloway in one field, the neighbor running Guernsey's, some Jersey's and brown Swiss. Polled steers and heifers scratch themselves against barns and disintegrating stalls. Calving time soon; quite a few cows lumbering swelled and slow near a crib of sere fodder. There's a turkey vulture sitting on Ethans' fence post next to the road; his curved beak and peering eyes make him look demonic. I've seen one with a six-foot wingspan trying to take off with a possum dangling in his claws. Formidable looking creatures, these raptors. Collif Deihl told me a story about a vulture that carried off a stillborn calf. It's hard to believe, but not impossible. There must be some truth to it; that's the way stories get started.

The weather is wet, a drizzle like thin soup. We can work in this, maybe get out today. Clark should be down about noon tomorrow to inspect the installation. Something to look forward to. My heron's in his spot. He hasn't moved for two days. His neck droops to the ground, but as I approach he looks up without raising his head. He looks me through, right through with a wet look of concern. He seems to think I'm troubled. It's our agreement, to watch out for one another. I smile for him, to show him I'm all right, haven't a care in the world, couldn't be happier to be alive. He doesn't buy the charade. The heron knows about solitude. The heron knows about suffering. Trucks going the other direction blast past me, raising water around their wheels and throwing it outward into the culvert. The heron stands rigid, in his frozen profile, and follows my eyes with his. I must turn my attention to the road, but he continues to watch the rear of my truck. I can't see this, from the cab, but I know it to be true.

There are instances in my life when relationships become absolutely clear. Words vanish and another kind of knowledge, a nebulous grokking, replaces them. It's happened to me three times that I can remember; it happened last night. I woke this morning sad, my first thoughts of Janelle, my mind unhampered by the minutiae of the day's responsibility. I felt a desolate peace, the peace that balances joy and sorrow: the balance peace of grokking. I rose to my peace and though Janelle entered my mind, she did so with slanting inconsequentiality. She merely glazed the surface. I let her go. I let her float out of myself, my body relinquishing the feel of her pale skin on my stomach, her odor and her taste; tactile familiarity became memory. Solitude filled the spot that was us. Wanting rose in my throat. I became a little melancholy, like the heron. He knows disintegration and wanting. That is why the heron watches the rear of my truck. We are brothers in the strata of solitude, bearing the interminable wanting, and together we wait. With time the wanting recedes, like a seasonal low tide lapping at the shore, but the waiting continues. It never goes away. It's always there, just beneath the surface. Blame the moon, urban pressure, hormones or premenstrual stress; sometimes the wanting overcomes the civil boundaries of sublimation. It turns man into beast.

I'm the first to the site. I survey the grounds, check to see if any of the boxes or the roll of wire I secreted beneath a pittosporum hedge have been stolen. Someone has driven spinouts in the lawn. They ran directly over a young almond, scalping one side, laying the bark open to the raw cambium. I'm afraid it won't make it. One valve box is crushed, dragged part way across the lawn. Unfortunately it's a big box, one of the expensive ones. I won't be responsible for the vandalism; the good Mormons will have to absorb the loss. We can work around it until lunch. I'll pick up a box then and add it to the bill. No other obvious damage; no broken lines, all the brass heads are still in place, the wire is still hidden. It must have been some teenagers bored with a lonely weeknight and charged by the waxing moon. Or the wanting overcame them: It spares not even the young.

After work, I think I'll clip some flowering quince, maybe some true jasmine. Do something in the spirit of ikebana, a windswept asymmetrical form, place it alongside my lamp in the front room. Put it just off center, to the left, a piece of obsidian between it and the lamp. Pretend I'm wholly fulfilled, taking the world in stride, absolved of wanting. That should get me back on track. It's a good day for banana fish. Then I'll call Janelle just to say "Hey."

Terry and Kevin arrive in Terry's microbus. They're eyes are red and dilated. No doubt they blew a bad boy on the ride up. Jesus H Christ. Youth. They mill around, talk briefly and I get them fitting control boxes. I want to have Mark finalize the heads, so that we can run the system when the head cheese arrives. It's always nice to show off a little, when you finish a job.

47

No Mark, and it's after nine. I check the guys, and head uptown to call. This is odd, Mark's my best worker, I give him more responsibility than the others. He usually gets to the site before I do. I pick up a new valve control box, and stop at a gas station to use the phone. No answer at Mark's place. I call Janelle. She sounds strained.

"Hello, Janelle, how are you."

"It's you, what are you doing calling me?"

"I wanted to talk with you."

"You never call me."

"That's not true. I called you Monday."

"You never call me. I always call you."

I can hear customers in the background, muffled voices and the sound of the radio.

"I've got customers. I have to go."

"All right. I'll stop by your house tonight to see you."

"No, don't."

She says this quickly, almost panicked.

"What's the matter?"

"Nothing. I have to go."

"Bye."

The line goes dead. I try Mark again and still there's no answer. Back at the church, the guys have finished the boxes and are standing around by the microbus. We do some general cleanup and fool around with the clock, running the syringe cycle and adjusting heads. At lunch, Kevin tells me he has to get back to town by two. He's riding with Terry, so they both want to leave early. It's all right; I can finish what needs to be done if I stay late. When we get back to the church I have them dig up and repair a leaking pipe, and then they leave. I'm gluing the final fittings when the head cheese arrives. I need one more piece so I can't demonstrate the system. We make an appointment for Friday morning at ten. I explain about the time clock, how to switch it on and off, and the times I've programmed for spring irrigation. He stays just long enough to hear the short explanation and leaves. It's about four. I'm concerned about Mark. This is unusual. I'll stop by his house on my way home. Maybe there will be a note. As I'm pulling out of the parking lot he pulls in. We both stop and talk across the doors of our cars.

The first thing he says is that he's in love. He tells me about this woman he's met and the terrific sex they had. He's so full of himself that I can't reprimand him for failing to show. We talk, he has a six pack, so we park, stand in the street and drink a beer. He apologizes and promises to make it up to me. I'm happy for him, really. Mark's pretty shy around women, and he's been single as long as he's worked for me. He says he'll come up tomorrow and help me finalize things. We part friends.

On my way home I stop for beer. Two girls are standing outside the liquor store. They come over to my truck and ask me to buy them beer. Cute figures, tight jeans and leather jackets, their hair cropped short at the neck and hanging over their eyes in front. Must be around sixteen. I eye them and my mind drifts to beaches, hot tubs, nubile prurient pleasure. They're almost legal: I must be nuts.

Someone has parked in my stall at the apartment but it doesn't matter. I park in front and walk upstairs. It feels good to be tired, walking the comfortable walk of loose, sore muscles. I'm a little dirty, but it's good honest grime from an honest day's work. That's what made this country; guys willing to work, labor, day in and day out. Not afraid to bust butt for a wage. They don't teach you that in college. Seems they forget about real labor. Everyone wants to be a manager, or spend their time shuffling papers and complaining about how tough it is. I know, I've done my college experience, took my degree in botany, even put some of it to use in selecting plants for the landscapes we install. Any idiot can plant something, but what you plant has to be right for the climate, the soil, the location. I use a lot of low maintenance plants. Most of my clients are retired, and they want a yard that's pretty to look at and not too difficult to maintain. Who can blame them; you spend half your life mowing and trimming, why should you retire to do the same? I can't fault their thinking.

*   *   *

I over sleep in the morning and drive straight to the sight. I watch for my heron, but he's not in his usual spot. The cattle are under some tangled oaks, a good distance from the highway. I think of the heron, where he's gone, why he's broken our pact. It makes me feel as though I've been abandoned. He was alone and he's disappeared. It worries me.

Mark's there, at the church, leveling the new control box. He's all smiles. We talk about his new girl. I smile and try to be cheerful, but he sees through me. I tell him about Janelle. I admit I really screwed up. He offers his sympathy and I feel bad all over again. Then we go to work.

The head cheese arrives on time. I run the system and he's impressed. The only complaint he has is about the wiring on the roof. He wants me to tuck it under the eaves in one spot. I agree. He says that he'll okay payment and the check will be in the mail today. I've heard that before, but don't make a remark.

Mark gets the ladder and then goes to gather tools. I climb to the roof and crawl to the edge. I lie on my stomach, thinking of Janelle, spreading my feet for balance and lean a good part of me over the edge of the roof to tuck the wiring. The wiring goes in easily without struggle. It goes in naturally, one loop after another, I continue pushing it in. Grab a section, hold on, push it in, over and over. Then Janelle's right in front of me, thrusting her hip, pointing her big finger like an elementary school teacher. I smell her skin, hear her voice, remark the way she holds her elbows splayed, like a ballerina. I feel so awful, thinking of her, that I want to moan. I don't know how, but I lose my concentration, lose my purchase, slide off the roof. One second I'm pushing wire into the eaves, the next I'm on the ground. Mark helps me up. I can stand, but my foot is already beginning to swell. I hobble to the truck, placing some weight down to test the foot. Nothing's broken, that I can tell, but it will lay me up for a few days. Mark leaves and I manage to drive home. About five miles from town are two white herons floating on the wind. They hold nearly motionless, making slight, quick adjustments to the angle of their wings. One drops, lower and lower, until I think it will land. It holds there, just for a second and turns to look at me. It is my friend. There is no mistaking those deep eyes, the sympathy in his face, the absoluteness of his stare. I see concern in his eyes, but I do not fake joy. He double droops his neck and lifts into the wind. I watch as they turn together and fly west.

Holy Spirit Conquest

I stood surrounded by Episcopal campers as the old man waved a bony arm out the side glass, bit down on the big block and slew gravel from the rear wheels into the pines. Ours was the hottest station wagon in the neighborhood and the only one, as far as I knew, with full flow headers, a shift kit and Holley carb. It was my job to collect the hubcaps sent spinning into front yards and driveways. To the old man, the Country Squire was more than a car; it was an expression of his automobile obsession. The Squire and a rusty English roadster sitting on jack stands in our small Boston Avenue garage filled his weekends. He was a real car nut.

"Good God," said a frosted-haired woman wearing gold toe sandals as the Ford hard-shifted, lurched sideways and spewed dust in the distance.

"428 cubic inches," I said proudly and pushed my polar sunglasses with the homemade side shields up on my nose. "With a Holley."

We followed camp counselors past the shower house to rectangular, forest green cabins. My friend John James was a Wolf and I was a Cougar, which hardly seemed fitting for a mountaineer so I changed it to Leopard like the legendary Snow Leopard of the mighty Himalayas rarely seen by anyone. Across the creek were Foxes. A blond girl in a tight, blue tee shirt smiled at me with perfect white teeth. I stood up as straight as I could, hunched my Trapper Nelson rucksack higher on my back and showed her my mountaineer's grin with the chipped incisor.

The cabin had beat up chairs and a wooden table in the center, two bunk beds in rooms on each side, and a glassless window with shutters that you could close from inside. Dennis introduced himself as our counselor, had us pick out a bunk and read us our schedule: Morning prayer in Holy Spirit Chapel at 7:30, breakfast, group activity before and after lunch and then introspection until dinner. After dinner, free time until dark and then the camp bonfire. A hike around the lake was scheduled for Tuesday, camp Olympics Thursday and a talent show on Friday night. Dennis said he'd be back before dinner and asked our names. In the bunk beneath me was a big guy with yellow teeth named Stu Stubman who already had a beard. There were twin albino brothers named Carlson and Carlton in the bunks opposite so I named them both Carl, just because, and a stocky boy in the other room named Johnny LePointe holding a bible who said "Praise Jesus" after every sentence. He gave me the evil eye behind prescription eyeglasses and called me Brother John and didn't like me already, so I changed my name to Jack, like Jack Whittaker, the famous Washington mountaineer and conqueror of Everest as well as the founder of Recreation Equipment where I got my trusty Silva Pathfinder compass and real leather mountaineer boots.

I stepped out the door, untangling the lanyard of the Silva and there she was, sitting on a tree stump with her long blond hair draped over one shoulder.

"Hello there," she said in a deep throaty voice, squaring her shoulders and pushing very definite breasts against the tight, blue tee shirt. I may have been only 14 but I knew solicitation when I heard it.

"Hi," I said.

"Hello Sweetheart."

Standing directly behind me was Stu, a lopsided grin on his big face, rocking from foot to foot in unlaced Converse high tops and tugging at the brim of a baseball cap with a bow-tied bunny on the brim.

"What's Cooking Good Looking?"

I checked the Silva co-ordinates and faced South, South-East toward the lodge.

"My name's Jill. I'm a Fox."

"Jack," I said. "I'm a going to be a famous mountaineer."

"My father has two girlfriends," Jill said.

"Like the legendary Sir Edmund Hillary," I said.

"Where we going?"

Jill put her arm in mine and turned to Stu.

"Jack and I are taking a walk," she said.

I pulled my arm away and caught it in the lanyard around my neck. The Silva flipped up and banged against my homemade polar sunglasses and lodged on the leather side shield. Stu shrugged his shoulders, rolled his eyes and then winked as he waddled toward the Wolf's cabin.

"What are you doing?" Jill said.

"Orienteering," I said and looked into Jill's perfect, white smile.

"Why?"

"The formidable Mt. St. Helens: My first conquest."

"The what?"

"Mt. St. Helens. 9,677 ft. Though not the highest mountain on the North American continent, Mt. Whitney is the highest, a challenging pinnacle in the range of volcanic peaks that comprise the well respected Cascade Range."

"You want to go down to the lake?"

She stared at me squarely, making her eyes go big and round, put both her silky smooth arms through one of mine and pulled hard against my shoulder.

"Sure," I stammered.

She shook her long hair, sighed and pulled closer, digging her bra and the very definite breasts into my bare arm. The tops of my feet started to itch and I looked down at my bulging trail shorts and tried not to think about Jill's breasts and prayed Dear God Not Now Make Me Normal and asked for some sort of sign. Jill reached up and pressed soft, moist lips against my ear.

"And you can be my boyfriend," she breathed.

*   *   *

I slipped out of my sleeping bag already dressed and tiptoed outside in wrinkled shirt and trail shorts. It was dark in the forest but the sun already showed on the snow-capped peak of the formidable Mt. St. Helens. I double laced my leather mountaineer boots, a trick experienced mountaineers used when descending precipitous routes. Morning prayer was my only obstacle so I couldn't waste any time. The trailhead of the southern route was four miles away and reconnaissance was required. For tomorrow's assault, I planned to start at 2 AM, the exact same time as the legendary Sir Edmund Hillary and his loyal sherpa Tensing

Norgay started when they courageously summited the challenging Mt. Everest from Camp IX. At home I had a ragged-edged copy of the July 13, 1953 Life Magazine with the cover photo of Hillary and Norgay and the account of their monumental conquest. I found it at a garage sale when I got the Nelson. I looked at my wristwatch, checked the Silva and removed my mountaineer's spiral notebook.

"Where you going?"

Stu stood on the cabin steps, wearing his hat, baggy maroon sweatpants, a faded gray tee shirt, saggy socks and big feet.

"For a hike," I answered and turned away to orient the Silva. "I don't have time for chit chat."

Stu scratched at his chin stubble, yawned and rubbed the thick, brown mat of hair on his head with the brim of his cap.

"Let me get my shoes," he said.

We hiked Holy Spirit Road and turned North North-West along the highway. I set a fast pace, hoping to discourage Stu so that he would turn back and leave me alone. He was not much of a hiker, with his big feet slapping at the ground and the way he rocked side to side, but he kept up. We stopped along the highway and leaned against the guardrail.

"So what are you in for?" Stu asked, reversing his cap.

"What do you mean?"

"Nobody volunteers for church camp. Me, my mother says I'm obsessed with sex but I saw it as a good business opportunity. How about you?"

"I'm a mountaineer. Holy Spirit is base camp for my conquest of the formidable Mt. St. Helens. Though not the highest mountain on the North American continent, Mt. Whitney is the highest, a challenging pinnacle in the range of volcanic peaks that comprise the well respected Cascade Range."

"You a Boy Scout?" he asked. I checked my wristwatch: 33 minutes, thought about making a notation and looked at the ground.

"I got kicked out on my first campout," I said and looked up at Stu's big face.

"How come?"

"Some of us beat up the Scoutmaster's kid."

"You beat him up?"

"I sort of watched. It wasn't just me."

Stu studied my face, put his hands in the front of his baggy maroon sweatpants, did a quick knee dip, and then broke into his lopsided grin.

"Cool!"

"I'm still going to be a mountaineer," I said. "It's what I've wanted my whole life."

Stu kept smiling, nodding his big head and then scratching his chin stubble.

"Blondie really goes for you, I can tell. She wants your bone."

I shrugged my shoulders and started hiking. Stu followed and didn't say anything until we stopped at the trailhead. I checked my wristwatch: another 26 minutes.

"She wants your bone, bad, you know," Stu panted with both hands on his knees. "She's ready."

"I'm a mountaineer," I said.

"You're going to get lucky."

We started up the trail, hiking through tall pine trees to an opening. Stu stopped beside me and we stood looking up at the summit. I'd thought about climbing Mt. St. Helens all summer, and here she was (mountaineers always call mountains she when they talk about conquests). I checked my watch: total time 67 minutes. I could probably get here faster without Stu. Above us, Dog's Head, partially covered in snow, glistened in the sunshine. Above that, the route to the summit was visible, but it didn't look anything like the southern route in the photographs of the challenging Mt. Everest and I was a little disappointed. Then Stu let out a formidable, wet fart, jerked his head around and looked behind us.

"You didn't get hurt, did you?" he asked with his lopsided grin and yellow teeth and we both laughed and stared at the mountain. I imagined what it would feel like to finally be on top. I was well prepared; training by climbing trees at the park, hiking up and down Boston Avenue wearing the Nelson loaded with three, full, one-gallon bleach bottles. For a final test, I wanted to hike the entire length of Dravus Avenue, a street so steep we never tried to ascend it in my mom's Mercedes diesel. However, getting to and from Dravus Avenue was a formidable problem. Like the legendary Sir Edmund Hillary said, one just had to pray to God for strength and rise to the challenge. We mountaineers are very religious when it comes to conquest.

"I've seen a lot of naked girls," Stu said. "I got magazines at home and a bunch at the cabin."

His big face was dripping sweat and I felt a little guilty for hiking so fast and trying to make him turn back. Then he smiled at me like I was his best friend and I tried to smile back like a mountaineer.

"Cool tooth," he said. "Makes you look . . . notorious. Notorious Jack."

I kept smiling and looked up at the sun shining on the summit.

"My mom says it's my idiot's grin."

Stu nodded.

"How do you get them?" I asked.

"Monthly subscriptions and a post office box," he answered. "A man can't be in business without a post office box."

"Is that what your old man does?"

"I don't have one."

I stood quietly, not sure of what to say. I oriented the Silva and checked my wristwatch, again. Three whole minutes lost to chit chat but I didn't want to mention it.

"What kind of business?"

"Sales," he said. "You're a mountaineer. I'm a salesman." He winked and stood up straight. "And a muffin diver," he said and the lopsided grin filled his big, sweaty face.

I got out my mountaineer's spiral notebook and made the notations: Time, date, bearing; estimated temperature and elevation.

"We better get back. I don't want to be late for chapel."

Stu nodded his head, reversed his cap back to normal and lead us down the trail raising clouds of dust beneath his big, slapping feet.

Getting back took longer even though we didn't stop for chit chat. I checked my wristwatch as we turned onto Holy Spirit Road but didn't want to take the time to make a notation. Beneath the camp signboard, a blue Chevy pickup truck stopped beside us. Inside the cab, a guy with a thick, red beard that covered his whole face leaned across the seat.

"You boys heading for camp?"

We both nodded.

"Get in," he said.

I climbed in first and then Stu. Stu had to pull his knees up against the dashboard because the seat was so far forward. The bearded guy put the truck in gear and it lurched forward, sputtered, and accelerated weakly.

"What you got under the hood?" I asked.

The bearded guy looked his eyes sideways at me without turning his head.

"Shit. Straight six."

"We got a big block," I said and pointed at the engine. "With a Holley."

"Rick," he said, showing crooked teeth behind the beard and sticking out his hand. "Holy Spirit maintenance."

We shook and he pulled a pack of Marlboros from his shirt pocket. He stuck one in his mouth and offered the pack my direction. I shook my head and Stu reached across, grabbed the pack, took one out and reversed his cap.

"I wanted a cowboy ever since I woke up," he said, and expertly tamped the cigarette on the back of his hand.

"Coming from the girl's camp or ditching morning prayers?" Rick asked as he folded a paper match backwards from a matchbook and scraped it against the striker with one hand.

"You can ditch morning prayers?" I asked.

"There's a girl's camp?" Stu asked.

We both stared at Rick, laughing at us and driving with one hand, the burning match almost to the edge of the book. He lit his cigarette, shook out the match just before it ignited the matchbook and passed it to Stu.

"This must be your first time," he said. "You boys don't know nothing."

Rick dropped us at the chapel. Episcopal campers were gathered at the double doors, filing into the rows of wooden benches on each side of the aisle, avoiding the front pews and bunching together near the back.

"Hello inmates," Stu said and winked at me. "Guess we made it in time."

He stomped past me down the aisle, hitching up his baggy maroon sweatpants and nodding his big head at Foxes. He stopped beside Jill's row and squeezed in beside her. I looked around at the inmates and then followed. Johnny LePointe gave me the evil eye behind his prescription eyeglasses and then pressed his palms together to pray. He wore a white, short-sleeved button down shirt with initials above the pocket. Jill moved over so that I could sit between her and Stu. A bald headed priest was standing in the pulpit, introducing himself as Father Joley and welcoming everyone to camp. He swept his beady eyes over the congregation, stopped to stare right where we were sitting until Stu took off his cap. Jill grabbed my hand when we kneeled to pray and held it between her legs. The tops of my feet began itching so I put my other hand in my pocket and tried to concentrate on my conquest. I felt my bone against my trail shorts and prayed Dear God Not Now Not Here Make Me Normal. When we sat up I pulled away my hand and she kissed me quickly on the cheek. Jill saw my bulging trail shorts and laughed into her cupped hands which made me angry but distracted my bone. Father Joley kept the service short, skipping the singing stuff, offered a camp blessing and then everybody had to file past him on the chapel steps. Stu shook his hand enthusiastically, congratulating him on the service and stood beside me smelling like cigarette smoke in his baggy, maroon sweat pants. I watched the backs of Dennis and a wide-hipped female counselor heading toward the lodge, and the inmates returning to their cabins.

"Gotta park a load," Stu said, winked and walked off toward the shower house. Jill started toward her cabin behind the other Foxes.

"See you at breakfast, lover," she called out. Father Joley turned quickly around, bored his beady eyes into me and appraised my wrinkled clothing. I ducked my head as if I hadn't seen his stare and headed for the cabin without looking back.

The Carls had playing cards with naked girls on them spread across the old wooden table.

"Where've you been?" they asked in unison. "Dennis was looking for you."

I rummaged in the Nelson for my bath towel and wash kit stuff sack.

"I went for a hike."

"He's Mr. Hiker," Johnny LePointe snickered from the next room. "Praise Jesus."

"You're in trouble," the Carls chimed.

I smiled at them like I didn't really care.

"Where'd you get the cards?"

They both looked sheepishly at each other.

"Stu left them," one of the Carls said.

"He left them?"

"Yeah," the other Carl said. "He has magazines, too," and his face began to redden from his forehead to his cheeks. It crept outward to his ears and then his nose and even his lips turned bright red. It looked like his face would explode with redness. He glanced around the cabin and lowered his head.

"*For sale,*" he whispered.

66

I grabbed my bath towel and wash kit stuff sack and went to the shower house. The inside was filled with smoke. The showers were empty but a stall door at the end of the row swung open and Stu stepped out.

"That's better," he said and smacked his stomach. "I wonder what's for breakfast."

"You've been smoking in here."

Stu nodded his head up and down with his lopsided grin, spread his arms like he was taking a standing ovation and belched.

"I feel great."

I tucked the Silva in my shirt and began washing. Stu borrowed my soap, splashed water on his face, and scrubbed at his cheeks and chin.

"Got any toothpaste?"

I pointed to my wash kit stuff sack and Stu squirted a thick bead of toothpaste on his finger and stuck it in his mouth. He rubbed enthusiastically and rinsed, hitched up his baggy maroon sweat pants and smiled at the mirror.

"The ladies love my smile," he said, admiring his yellow teeth.

I looked at my broken incisor and practiced my mountaineer's grin.

"Looking good, Notorious Jack," he said and clapped me on the back. "You're ready for blondie, now. She wants you."

"You think so?"

"Man, you're in," Stu said. He put his hands together at his mouth like a megaphone and quietly mouthed, "SHE WANTS YOUR BONE."

"Uh, I don't know."

"You're going to get lucky."

Stu sat back against the sink, yanked down his faded gray tee shirt and crossed his big feet. He stuck his hand in the front of his baggy maroon sweat pants and did the quick knee dip and then rubbed at his forehead. I folded my towel and washcloth, and checked my wristwatch.

"You've never done it, have you?" he asked.

"I'm going to be in high school next year, you know."

"I've got magazines back at the cabin."

I packed my things into my wash kit stuff sack and avoided Stu's eyes.

"Then what's the matter?"

"This is church camp."

Stu blinked, threw back his head and exhaled loudly. He crossed his arms and stared at me like he was astonished.

"All you have to do is close the deal."

He nodded his head up and down enthusiastically

"I'm a mountaineer," I said.

"It's going to happen. No parents around to get in the way. The deal is pending," he said and nodded his head.

"But church camp?"

"It's . . . preforedained," he said. "God wants you to get lucky."

We left the shower house and walked toward our cabin.

"Call my man Mr. Lucky, he's in business now," he said and started laughing and then I started laughing, too. He punched my shoulder and gave me a shove.

"Hey, where'd you get the cigarette?"

Stu stopped, gave me the astonished look again and pulled Rick's cowboys and matches from beneath his cap.

"Momma didn't raise no fool."

*   *   *

After breakfast, the Wolves went to Spirit Lake for canoeing and the Cougars got group activity: plastic trash bags for camp cleanup with a reward for the one who brought in the most litter. It's surprising how many wrappers, cigarette butts and cans you can find in the woods. Mountaineers call the South Col on Mt. Everest the highest dumpsite in the world because it's littered with empty oxygen bottles, torn up pieces of tents, food tins and abandoned cooking gear. At 26,000 feet, nobody got group activity but you had to eat. I knew all about it. I had invested my entire camp allowance on freeze-dried meat, powdered soup and a Primus white gas stove with cooking set identical to the one Colin Fletcher used in The Complete Walker. Colin may be just a hiker but he has a lot of good advice for us mountaineers. I wandered around the restrooms, past the empty Foxes cabin and down to Spirit Lake. Not far from the docks, Stu lounged with a cigarette. I dropped my trash sack beside his.

"Hey Stu."

"Notorious Jack."

I walked to the shoreline, located the girl's camp across the lake and checked the Silva. East South-East. I took out my mountaineer's spiral notebook and made a notation. Around the end of the docks, Wolves paddled canoes, taking turns while the counselors shouted instructions. I picked out John James. He wore patterned shirts without buttons or collars that his mom sewed for him. I got a look down her blouse once and she wasn't wearing a bra. My mom said she liked her because she was a hippy.

Two motorboats filled with Foxes idled offshore near the docks. Stu came over beside me with the cigarette hidden in his palm.

"Sitting on a million bucks and they don't even know it," he said and shook his head.

The Foxes noticed us and Jill jumped up in a yellow bikini and orange life jacket and waved. The boat made another circle and all of a sudden Jill dropped her life jacket and dove into the water. The counselor in the boat yelled at her but she was a strong swimmer. She emerged from the lake in bright sunshine, water streaming off her smooth skin and long blond hair like a holy vision and ran over to me and wrapped her arms around my neck.

"I got you something," she said, breathing heavily and squashing the Silva against my chest so that it hurt.

"See?"

She rocked away, threw back her head and closed her eyes. Around her neck was a medal on a thick silver chain but I could see almost all her very definite breasts.

"I made them use a different chain," she said. "The other one was too feminine for a hiker."

"Mountaineer," I corrected as the tops of my feet started to itch. She twisted around and lifted her hair off her neck.

"Go ahead, unhook it."

I fumbled with the tiny latch and finally the chain came apart and Jill held the medal in her hand.

"It's Saint Christopher," she said. "To protect you."

She reached around my neck, fastened the latch and pressed her wet pelvis hard against me. "For your conquest," she said in the throaty voice. I prayed Dear God Not Now Please Please Not Now because my feet itched like crazy and I knew that she could feel my bone.

"Where'd you get it?" I stammered, as she made her eyes go big and round and then pressed against me even harder.

"I bought it at the girl's camp" she whispered in a voice filled with lust.

She looked at Stu and the cigarette and let go of me. I put my hands in the pockets of my bulging trail shorts and started bouncing up and down.

"Oh just one drag, *darling*," she said in a phony accent. "I've been *dying* for one all day."

Stu let her have the cigarette and she held it in front of her with her back to the lake, the cigarette poised naturally between two fingers. She took a deep drag and exhaled smoke over her head.

"You're a love," she said, confidently flicked the ash and handed Stu the cigarette.

"Come on. We have to convince the counselors why I just had to jump off that boat or they'll make me wash dishes. We can talk our way out of it, I know. I do it all the time."

We walked toward the boat docks and when I looked back Stu was pumping his fist and smiling his lopsided grin. Giggling Foxes in towels ran from the boat docks toward their cabin. One tall Fox slyly smiled at me as she approached. She wore a red, one-piece bathing suit with one shoulder strap hanging loose off her shoulder. She passed slowly and flipped her long, dark hair.

"Bitch," Jill sneered.

The wide-hipped, female counselor was standing at the edge of the docks.

"Miss Devine, you owe me an explanation."

"I'm sorry, I really am, Betty. But when I saw my fiancé on the beach I was overcome." Jill grabbed my arm and pressed her face against my cheek. The tops of my feet began to itch and I tried to think up a quick prayer.

"I am Ms. Johnson, to you, Miss Devine. I was Ms. Johnson to you last year and I am Ms. Johnson to you this year. And this is not your fiancé."

Jill stepped back, her jaw hanging open and pressed both hands to her cheeks.

"Why Ms. Johnson, this *is* my fiancé. My parent's promised me to him. That's the way we people do it," she said and smiled her perfect teeth. I looked into her big, round eyes believing every word and almost forgetting I was going to be a mountaineer: There's nothing like a girl with long wet hair and very definite breasts in a yellow bikini to disrupt your focus. Ms. Johnson tightened her lips and narrowed her eyes. Jill put both her arms around mine and hugged herself close to me.

"I'm getting cold, honey. Ms. Johnson, may I go and get out of this wet suit? You wouldn't want me to catch a cold, would you?"

Ms. Johnson scowled and shook her head.

"Go on," she said and pointed her finger at Jill. "And this isn't over."

Jill kissed me quickly on the cheek.

"See you later, honey," she said, started off then stopped to blow me a kiss. Ms. Johnson turned her scowl on me and I tried to look as grownup as I could but I know I had my idiot's grin on my face. The sun burned onto my head as I squirmed and rubbed one foot on top of the other.

"I'll remember you," Ms. Johnson said and pointed her finger. "You go on, too."

I turned and walked back to Stu.

"Notorious Jack," he said, smiled and picked up our plastic trash bags. "Come on, I figured out how this business works."

We hiked through the woods, past the Cougar cabin and angled toward the lodge. Around back, Stu went to a wooden enclosure, opened the gate and pointed at a dozen trashcans lined up against the building. He lifted the lid from one, removed the bulging plastic trash bag and replaced it with his empty one. He handed it to me, took my plastic trash bag and repeated the same procedure. We circled around the lodge and emerged next to the shower house. Ahead in the opening, the Carls held up nearly empty plastic trash bags and Johnny LePointe stood proudly above three full plastic trash bags. Stu nodded at Dennis, a clipboard in hand, and held up his plastic trash bag. Dennis nodded back, put his hands on his hips and scowled at the Carls.

"What's your stories?"

They looked at each other and then one of the Carls spoke up.

"We aren't suppose to go into the sunshine."

Dennis stared at their pale faces for a few seconds and tapped his pencil on the clipboard.

"Huh. All right, all right. Good work, then."

He tapped his pencil on the clipboard again and turned to Johnny LePointe.

"Looks like we've got a winner," Dennis said. Johnny jumped into the air, clapped his hands and dropped to his knees, praising Jesus and all those who had left behind their litter. Dennis reached down and put his hand under his arm.

"That's great, Johnny, just great. Get up now. Everybody, put your sacks in the back of the truck over there and go wash. It's lunch time."

We carried our plastic bags to the Chevy and tossed them in the bed. Rick stepped from behind the cab, a cigarette in his mouth and looked at Stu.

"Hello boys. A little trash duty?" he asked. He took the cigarette from his mouth and stepped menacingly toward Stu. Rick was a short guy but stocky and a full-grown adult.

"Got a cigarette, Stu?" he asked and grabbed Stu's arm.

Stu pulled backwards and looked at me with panic in his eyes.

"NO, I DON'T HAVE A CIGARETTE," he yelled out. "I DON'T SMOKE." Dennis looked over as he was walking toward Holy Spirit Lodge.

"Hey, I told you boys get cleaned up for lunch." He gave Rick the evil eye and Rick dropped Stu's arm and rolled back on his heels. He leaned casually against the fender and narrowed his eyes at Dennis. Dennis took a step toward the truck.

"Any problems?" he asked.

Rick laughed low in his throat, took a long drag off his cigarette and climbed into the Chevy. He fired up the six and revved the motor.

"Get going. We've got canoeing at one," Dennis called to us. Rick jammed the Chevy into gear and dumped the clutch to spin the rear tires. Dennis walked over to where we were standing.

"Don't mind him. He's an asshole," he said and watched the Chevy swerve onto the road behind the lodge.

"Go on. It's lunch time."

Lunch was served in Holy Spirit Lodge on trestle tables. Wolves and Cougars sat at one line of tables; Foxes, Father Joley and the counselors at the other. Two women worked behind a steam table and served hot dogs, macaroni and cheese, and chili. One was really old, with gray, scraggly hair sticking through a net on her head and skinny arms that had veins poking out. She went back into the kitchen, carrying an empty serving tray and walking with a limp because she wore one of those shoes with the extra thick sole. The other was blond and pretty but not as pretty as Jill and the same age as the counselors. We finished and got in line to bus our trays. Jill squeezed in behind me and bumped me with her tray.

"What are you doing after lunch?" she asked.

"Canoeing," I said.

"We have to make garlands for the pews. I'd rather not be involved, *at all*."

I moved forward in line with my tray.

"You want to sneak off?"

"I don't know," I said.

"Come on, don't be a chicken," she said and pushed me in the back again. "Meet me in the chapel in ten minutes," she whispered. "Maybe you'll get lucky."

The tops of my feet began to itch and when I turned around I saw that Father Joley was joking with Foxes, jiggling a fork with a hot dog on it and waving a spoonful of macaroni in the other hand. He saw me and the smile disappeared from his face. He lowered the fork and spoon and crossed his arms over his fat stomach and made the beady eyes. John James in his collarless shirt got in line behind Jill.

"Notorious Jack," Stu said and put his tray on top of mine. He banged the Silva hanging from my neck but didn't notice. John James tilted his head with curiosity, mouthed 'Notorious Jack' and I just shrugged.

"Help me out here," Stu winked. "Salting the mine paid off."

He crossed the room and walked out of the lodge with the Carls, Johnny LePointe and three Wolves at his heels. I threw away the trash, put the utensils in a tub and stacked the trays on a wheeled cart. Jill did the same and then the Foxes gathered at one end of Holy Spirit Lodge with Father Joley and Ms. Johnson. Dennis waved me over to his table.

"Jack, I need your help," he said.

"Okay."

"I need you to get the Cougars together at the dock in about fifteen minutes."

"You mean the Leopards. We're the Leopards now, like the legendary Snow Leopard of the mighty Himalayas rarely seen by anyone."

"Huh?"

"The Himalayas. Home of the highest mountain range in the world, including the challenging Mt. Everest, first conquered by the legendary Sir Edmund Hillary and Tensing Norgay unless you believe that Mallory and Irvine actually reached the summit and vanished on their descent." I held up the Silva and pointed it across the room. "They were last sighted below the Second Step, you know."

"Uh huh …. Look, you've got a watch. Can you get the Cougars…."

"Leopards," I corrected.

"Right. Get the leopards to the dock in fifteen minutes?"

"Well…." I hesitated.

"Can you do that?"

I nodded and put on my homemade polar sunglasses.

"You make those little side shields on there?"

"Real leather," I said. "From our old dining room chairs. Already broken in."

Rick walked past, stroking his beard and not even looking at me or Dennis. He mumbled something under his breath and Dennis watched him all the way to the door.

"Fifteen minutes," he said to me and turned back to his food.

*   *   *

The bunk bed in the other room was covered with magazines. The Carls each had one and Johnny LePointe had two in one arm and was turning the pages of another on the bed. I stood in the doorway and waited for them to notice.

"That's the whole deal, right there," Stu said, pointing to a fold out. "Woman in all her glory."

"Glory to God," Johnny LePointe said and pushed his prescription eyeglasses up on his nose.

"That's right, my man. That's the way God made her and there's nothing to be ashamed of in that."

"Praise Jesus," Johnny LePointe said and handed Stu two five-dollar bills.

"Wait a minute. We haven't agreed on a price."

Johnny LePointe stepped back and looked at me. He stared for a second, his eyes big and wild behind the prescription lenses. Then he grabbed at his mouth and wiggled his finger at Stu.

"I'll pay the same as these. That's fair."

"Different deal," Stu said as he shook his head. "What you got is good, classic centerfold material. Regular price for each one. But this is a different deal. Pet of the

Year. Costs me more, I got to charge more. It's just business."

Stu looked my direction and winked, then nodded me over. Johnny LePointe was clutching the magazines to his chest, digging the ends into the skin of his throat. Stu pointed to the spread on the bunk bed.

"Collector's edition; Limited publication, only got one."

Johnny looked at me and grabbed at his mouth again. He started to whine softly through his nose and looked at me, then Stu, then down at the magazine. Stu closed the magazine and Johnny grabbed at it.

"That's all I've got. That's my whole allowance."

"Then I think I've got business with some Wolves."

Johnny looked at me with the wild eyes, the magazines gouging a red welt into his throat, and licked his lips.

"Okay, okay," he said. "I'll pay more. But it's my chapel money for God."

"He'd be happy for you," Stu said and winked. "And so am I."

Johnny went to his bunk, opened his Bible and pulled out a ten-dollar bill. Then he carefully arranged the magazines beneath his pillow. He pushed his sleeping bag over the pillow and put the bible on top. Stu folded the bills into a roll around his finger.

"Pleasure doing business with you, gentlemen," he said to the Carls. Stu grabbed his duffle bag, scooped up the magazines on the bunk bed and started for the door. "I've got business with some Wolves."

"Hey, we're suppose to be at the dock," I said and checked my wristwatch. "In six minutes."

"That should give me enough time to close the deal," Stu said and disappeared.

I watched the Carls leafing through their magazines and Johnny LePointe sitting on his bunk bed with his right hand on his bible. He looked at me with big, guilty eyes and then jumped to his feet and started out the door.

"Hey, where you going? We're suppose to be at the dock for canoeing."

Johnny LePointe stopped, hung his head and went back to his bunk bed. He removed the prescription eyeglasses and put his forehead in his hands.

"I did a bad thing," he muttered. "I need to go to chapel."

"We're suppose to go canoeing," I said.

Both Carls stood up and started for the door. They each wore visor caps with bandanas attached to the back that hung down and covered their necks.

"Okay," one of the Carl's said. "But I don't want to row."

"You don't row, you paddle," the other Carl said.

"I still don't want to do it."

They walked past me and then Johnny LePointe got up and followed. I watched them until they were out of sight and then headed for the chapel. Wolves were gathered around the shower house with mops and buckets and spray bottles. They sprayed their bottles at each other or into the air. A counselor yelled from inside and they went in. I crossed the open dirt to the chapel steps, looked behind me and took out my mountaineer's spiral notebook. I made an abbreviated entry for the occasion: time and date, only. No need for bearing or temperature, though my face was feeling hot and already the tops of my feet had begun to itch. Then I checked the Silva, anyway: Mt. St. Helens, North by North-West. Over the treetops she was like a vision, snow glistening in the sun on the summit, no evidence of strong wind blowing. Blowing is always a possibility with conquests. Sometimes you can't even stand and have to stay on your knees. By this time tomorrow my first conquest would be under my belt. I'd have to be careful; many mountaineers run into trouble after completing their conquest and submit to fatigue and want to just sleep. It was good to allow extra time for rest, even if it meant spending less time on top. I didn't want to get caught in an unpredictable situation.

"Don't be shy," came Jill's voice from the crack between the double doors. One door opened slightly and just her hand reached out. My feet really itched and my hands were nervous as I thought about Jill in her yellow bikini and very definite breasts and looked up at Mt. St. Helens fewer than four miles away. Mountaineer's need to stay focused about conquest regardless of distractions. Jill pushed open the door, grabbed my hand and pulled me inside. Bright sunshine poured in the windows and filled the chapel with light. Jill led me down the aisle, around the altar and through a single door into the vestry. She closed the door behind us and we stood in the darkness letting our eyes adjust. The small room was dimly lit by a narrow row of stained glass windows high on the wall. On one side was a closet, a floor to ceiling cabinet with a padlock, and in the middle of the room a small wooden table and chair. On the other side, beneath the windows, was a short sofa. Jill sat down on the sofa and I sat down next to her and tried to think about tomorrow's ascent.

"I knew you'd come," she whispered.

It was hot and very still in the room. Jill lay back on the sofa and pulled me down next to her. She started kissing me on the cheeks and ears and then she kissed me on the mouth and gave me the tongue. It was so hot I could hardly breath and my feet began to burn and my bone pushed at my trail shorts against her thigh. Her very definite breasts were right next to me and I kissed her back the way I'd seen it done on television but forgot to close my eyes. She took my hand and put it under the bottom of her tee shirt.

"You can touch them," she said and made her eyes big and round. "Go ahead."

I was breathing hard and fast and she was too and she pulled her tee shirt up so I could see and I slowly put my trembling hand around one breast. I closed my eyes and prayed "Dear God, Thank You," and pure, bright white light filled the room.

Jill sat up quickly, yanking her shirt down and twisting around on the sofa. My hand was caught and she pulled on my arm to get it out.

"Miss Devine," a voice said and I opened my eyes and Ms. Johnson and Dennis were standing in the doorway. Johnny LePointe tried to hide behind Father Joley but I could see his white shirt. Jill pushed me away from her and stood up.

"It was his idea," she said, pointing at me and shaking her hand. "He talked me into it," she said as she smoothed her tee shirt. I sat up, blinking at the bright, white light that was shining like a halo behind Jill's head.

"All right, Jack. What the hell's going on?" Dennis said.

Jill ran to Ms. Johnson and threw her arms around her wide hips and started to cry. She looked back at me with dry, narrowed eyes and I knew that I didn't mean a thing to her even if she had told Ms. Johnson I was her fiancé.

Father Joley stepped forward with his beady eyes and crossed his arms on his fat stomach.

"You can consider your stay at Holy Spirit terminated," he said and walked out of the room.

"You're in trouble," Johnny LePointe said.

Dennis frowned at me and held up his hand.

"Jack, get back to the cabin and stay there."

He followed Father Joley and Johnny LePointe and called after them in the chapel. Ms. Johnson took Jill by the shoulders and they marched out the door together and I was all alone, on the sofa, on my first full day of church camp feeling sick to my stomach and I was getting sent home. I got up and wandered back to the cabin and sat dejectedly on the bunk bed in the dim light. After a while, Stu came in.

"Kicking me out," I said. "I screwed up."

I stared at the scuffed wooden floor.

"Tough break, Jack," he said.

"I could have conquered Mt. St. Helens," I pleaded. "But instead I went for the girl. I'm no mountaineer," I said and shook my head in disgust.

Stu shook his head, too, just to be helpful.

"Well, did you get lucky?" he asked hopefully

"I touched her breasts."

He nodded his head up and down thoughtfully. "I've never touched any."

I looked at him with surprise and he shrugged his shoulders.

"I'm a salesman," he said. "Closing the deal is the hardest part."

Dennis came in shaking his head and stood with his hands on his hips.

"Did what I could, but no luck," he said. "Father Joley already called your Dad. Better get packed up." He turned and left and Stu helped me get my things together. I filled the Nelson with my stuff and before I tied it shut Stu pulled the Pet of the Year Collector's Edition from his duffle bag and gave it to me.

"I have extra copies," he said and smiled his lopsided grin but I didn't feel any better. He grabbed my shoulder.

"You're still a mountaineer; you just had a bad break. The deal's not over, *it's pending.*"

I held the magazine up to the light. The girl on the cover had long, blond hair hiding very definite breasts and wore a yellow bikini. She stared with perfect white teeth and wide eyes. I handed it back to Stu and picked up the Nelson.

"Just a bad break, huh?" I asked.

"I'm a salesman," Stu said and nodded enthusiastically.

"And I'm going to be a mountaineer," I answered.

Stu smiled his lopsided grin and punched me on the shoulder. I headed for the door.

"See you around?" he asked.

"Yeah," I answered as I walked out. Mt. St. Helens was shining tall and proud above the treetops in the afternoon sun. I checked the Silva and pulled out my mountaineer's spiral notebook and made a final notation. Not every ascent is successful. There were many attempts to conquer the challenging Mt. Everest before the summit was finally claimed. Like Stu said, the deal wasn't over; it was pending.

Working with Duane

We get along pretty well and everyone does his share except Gary; no one likes to be teamed with him. You have to work twice as hard and do the thinking for two and still hold your temper. He's a real pain in the ass.

We meet at Carlo's in the morning, load the truck and head for the installation site. Sometimes we'll get a big project, a couple months or so like last year, and then it's just regular labor. Get up, commute, and do the same thing over and over. Collect your check on Friday, go to the bank before it closes and rest your swelled feet and tired back until Monday. It's not what I want to do forever, but I don't have many options right now. I can't complain. Carlo's pretty good to us, he pays decently and I like most of the crew. It changes constantly; one week this guy will come on and the next it's someone else. That's the way it is with casual labor. Everybody's an independent contractor so Lou doesn't worry about taxes or Social Security deductions. We're supposed to handle that ourselves. Most guys fail to mention it, if you know what I mean.

Sonny's been around the longest. He's Carlo's youngest son and his real name's Alberto and he plans to take over when Carlo retires. He doesn't bother anyone much, but usually falls to it with the rest. Some days he'll loaf, push a broom or bitch about his wrist (he broke it a couple years ago) or even stand around and tell others what to do. We don't necessarily like it, but what can you do? He's the boss's son. No one really likes him so, it figures, he hangs with Gary. The rest of the core is Kenny and me. Kenny's a failed, basketball hopeful. He was doing real well, high scorer in his junior year in high school, leading his team to the state championship and then he mangled his knee so badly that he couldn't play. It seemed to discourage him from everything and he's been working with us ever since. His teammate and best friend Duane played senior year, became the high scorer, and goes to Coast Community. If he does well this season, he'll probably get a scholarship to Bakersfield. A scout already talked to him. He's only working with us while he waits for the season to begin. He's the nicest black guy I ever met. Duane reads a lot, like me, so we get along. I like to give him books from my collection that I know he'll enjoy. He appreciates it and always returns them undamaged. We're the same, that way. I like Kenny, too, but whenever he returns a book it's trashed and I know he didn't read it.

The thing I like most is the talk. Sonny talks about what happened on television the night before or some really dumb movie that he liked and Carlo's kind of the same. They play golf and live to eat big meals. Sonny carries about twenty-five extra pounds around the middle. I saw him with his shirt off once and around his waist it looked like the cellulite women get on their thighs. He's been fat for as long as I can remember, so I guess it seems natural to him. I'm just the opposite, lean and rangy, so maybe that's why it strikes me as unusual. They do pretty well for themselves. Sonny still lives at home. His mom cooks and does laundry and even makes his bed. We tease him about it, but I don't know if that's really bad; I mean, if my mom would do all that stuff for me, I wouldn't turn it down.

Kenny and Duane are my best friends even though we don't hang out much. They get into some wild things. Kenny can go out and party with some woman or two or three and show up Carlo's without ever getting any sleep. He tells wild stories. I want him to write them down sometime, but he says I do all the reading so I should write them. Some day I might.

Duane is cool. He's about six three, goes maybe one

seventy-five; he's built how a good point guard should be. I can imagine him directing traffic on the fast break, faking a pass and pulling up for a jumper at the foul line. He plays in a summer league to stay in shape and that's what we talk about the most; Duane lives for playing ball. It's his thing. He could make it to the pros if he wants it bad enough, but he says he's not counting on anything. He's a college man, too. Studies business, at Coast, and figures if he has to he could get a degree and go into management. Something with sports. He'd be successful at it, you can tell. He has that calm assurance guys have who've been something, somewhere. I really like him. You can joke with him about being black and he'll come right back at you with a big smile and some smart-ass, white honky privilege line, of his own. It's like he's not any different; he doesn't talk jive or carry an attitude or walk like some black guys. It's good to meet a guy like that. It puts all your prejudices out the door where they belong. For instance, this guy Ron we call Rock Man, because his thing is freebasing, was working with us on and off. He's black, too, but really black. He walks like he's always stepping over something with one foot. When he talks it's always ghetto, never good English, and he wears a do-rag even when it's hot as hell. He puts on the whole thing, talking about his bitches, strutting with his weird walk, and singing rap to himself in the back seat of Carlo's truck. It's funny to see him with Duane. They act different. It makes me like Duane all the better.

I'll give you an example of what I mean. Last month we had a three-day assembly at a building in Industry. We didn't know where we were going, so we showed up at the truck in our usual worn-out jeans and stained tee shirts. I wear boots because my feet have no arch and I need ankle support if I'm going to be standing all day. Kenny has these worn-through basketball high-tops that smell like cat shit; they really do. Carlo won't let him wear them in the truck. He has to take them off and put them in the bed or sit back there himself. Even with that you can still smell them if we get stopped in traffic and it's hot. We pile in and make our obligatory stop for coffee. It's about an hour to Industry. The whole time Rock Man's leg is bouncing and he's rapping. And he sniffles all the time. It drives me nuts. I don't know how the others put up with it. He wears mirrored sunglasses, too. With the do-rag and the shades, he looks kind of suspicious. We get to the site and put on our tool belts and hard hats - we have to wear hard hats now because of Carlo's liability - and go up to the third floor where we'll be doing the installation. Here we are dressed like shit, and the building's filled with good looking secretaries in skirts parading the halls or sitting at their desks. Of course Kenny about comes loose at that. If Ron's the Rock Man, Kenny's the puda man. He gets something out of every job we do. I told him once that pudenda is another word for pussy and he made it his own. Last year we did a two month installation at UCLA and after the second week he was banging this big brunette supervisor about forty-five in her office off and on during lunch. He's not particularly handsome and he's sure no gentleman, but women flock to him like crazy. I can't explain it. I figure most women have dirtier minds than men and got to be twice as horny. I never meet those types. It's either born again Christians or mousy virgins who live with their parents. It must be the glasses.

The office building is real nice. It has dark wood paneling and plants hanging in atriums. I can see it's going to be rough getting the material upstairs without damaging anything. Carlo sends Kenny and me down to the truck for his blueprints and to check if all the material's arrived. We're not supposed to have to hump it to the site, but usually the truck driver just dumps it somewhere inconvenient and leaves. It can be a real mess. We cover the PO and everything's there and I grab the blueprint from the front seat. Coming up the service elevator, we can hear shouting somewhere in the office. When we round the corner to where we'll be working, the Rock Man's in the corner and he's pulled a switchblade on Carlo. A bunch of secretaries are against the other wall huddled around one gal who's crying. Duane's talking to rock man who keeps the blade up in the air swishing back and forth at arm's length. With the do-rag, shades and now a switchblade, he looks dangerous. Duane steps toward him talking him down and Rock Man takes a swipe at him. Duane backs off and he and Carlo stand watching him like a trapped animal until the police arrive. They pull a taser on him, drop him to the floor and haul him away. Carlo says he's their problem now and the girl he had been menacing or hitting on or something I never did find out goes with them to file a complaint. I remember as they take him out in bracelets, Duane watches and hangs his head like he's embarrassed. I know what he means. Sometimes, when you see some white guy do something awful it makes you ashamed. The Rock Man wants to come back to work for Carlo, but this was a month ago and we still haven't seen him. The crazy thing about it is, Carlo will probably let him.

Today's a special job and it will be just Kenny and Duane and me. Carlo's at his Saturday morning golf game and Sonny's gone to Vegas to try to break the bank. We're going to be working in the freezer at Dantel. I strap my tools to my Bonnie, run back to get a wool balaclava I bought especially for the first time we did this installation, and fire up. I really like riding a bike to work. It wakes you up in the morning. It's fun blasting along in the fast lane or splitting lanes when traffic's not moving. Everytime I get on and ride anywhere, I can't believe it's legal. I couldn't live without it. I dress really warm for this job; long underwear, turtleneck, flannel shirt, sweater and parka. The freezer's a bitch. They store high tech plastics inside and keep the temperature at zero degrees. It's supposed to be a dry freezer, no ice, but last time there was about half an inch of slush on the floor. There are fans running all the time in these big air conditioners that hang from the ceiling; that's where we'll be working. They want some grating beneath the air conditioning units so they can service them without bringing in hoists.

Kenny's car's in front of the guard's gate and Duane's driving. Kenny's stretched out in the passenger seat half asleep. I can see his hard hat pushed down over his eyes. We all wear them now, as a kind of joke. When we were doing a storage rack for GTE, Kenny found a labeling machine and everyone made a message for the back of their hard hats. Kenny's is "Live fast, die young, leave a lot of outstanding debts." I put "Is it Friday, Yet?" on mine but then I took it off. It wasn't funny like Kenny's.

We sign in and the guard lets us through. He says I have to leave the bike outside, so Kenny is forced to sit regular and I squeeze in the back. He looks like warmed over death: the death of the puda man. He isn't going to be much good today. We'll let him stay on the ground and hand up grating. Duane can be the new high-altitude man. Kenny and I pride ourselves on that. Whenever we're building pallet rack, or split level mezzanines, we do all the work up top. Walking two-inch beams twenty-two feet in the air is exciting stuff. You carry the next beam like a balance rod as you go before bolting it in place. I'm getting into rock climbing, so I feel pretty good about my balance. Kenny just seems to have no natural fear of falling. I think his good sense of balance comes from once being an athlete. Duane's never been up top in the freezer. He wasn't with us when we built this system. I don't know how he'll make out.

The freezer's closed up tight with big, galvanized-steel sliding doors. They're electronically controlled, with emergency overrides inside in case you get trapped. The only way you couldn't get them open would be if all power went out. Then the coolers would shut down, too. If you had to, you could survive it. I punch open the door and we push through the dirty transparent strips. They're supposed to keep in the cold when the doors are open and allow you to see inside but you can't see shit through them. The temperature's three degrees above zero at ground level and the top level's full of pallets. It's about thirty feet to the ceiling. The air conditioners hang down about four feet and are pretty long. We'll have to lay a lot of grating to provide any kind of platform. That means that we'll be inside all day. At least only one wall needs to be done. The other's behind a cyclone fence from top to bottom with combination locks and steel cage doors. No one gets in there for nothing.

Kenny goes to get a fork lift. Duane and I get out the PO, check the materials, unload our tools and flake out the extension cords. We have to Tec screw each section of grating to the pallet beams. They won't let us use cleats or just bolt the grating together. First we have to put in flat-channel and bolt those to the uprights. Then we add another upright to each channel and then I-beams along the back wall. That gives us something to lay the grating on. We'll short nail this job, like always, and bolt the grating together anyway. That way we only have to Tec screw every third or fourth piece, but it'll still be slow going no matter how you look at it.

Kenny comes back with this old guy, Tony's his name, on a fork lift. I forgot this was a union shop and pretty particular about how things are done. This guy gave us all sorts of trouble the last time we were here. Kenny's smooth talking him to start moving pallets while we bolt in flat-channel and uprights. I guess we get off on a better footing, because the guy seems willing enough to help out. Maybe it won't be so bad. We can get him unloading and by the time he's finished we'll have everything bolted in place. Then we'll toss up the grating and when we get it down on one side he can load that area while we start working on the other. Kenny gets him going and he's pretty good; he lifts things down with few moves and always blows his horn going through the transparent strips. Both me and Kenny have driven fork on jobs; Kenny's a little faster than me, but he almost always clips a wall or drops something. It's not difficult to do, but it's hard as hell to be quick and smooth.

Kenny's climbing anyway and we go up and Duane

tosses us flat-channel. We have to take off our gloves to put the bolts through and the nuts on. I drop quite a few in the process. After about thirty minutes I have to go outside to warm up. I get cold right down through my feet and when I come out into the sunshine my glasses fog up. I hate this goddamn freezer. We work in turns, going out to stand in the sun and then back up top. Kenny's got more meat on his bones so he doesn't seem to mind it as much as I do. It isn't long until we have the beams in place and can start installing grating. We're going to skip lunch and try to get through this by two o'clock. I don't like the idea, but the Kenny and Duane are for it so I go along. The grating's really sharp along the ends. They never cut it square, so there's always an edge that's dangerous as hell. Kenny laid his forearm open about forty stitches worth, once. Carlo had to take him to the hospital in the middle of the job. The rest of us just kept working. It wasn't unusual; someone almost always gets hurt on a job. I've been lucky. I watch myself and stay away from the new guys. They're the most dangerous. My only complaint is my hands. They get swelled and sore when we do shelving jobs and I have to carry a lot of posts. I probably have some arthritis, or something, but I don't like to think about it. It makes me feel like I'm working hard and getting nowhere.

The grating's not easy to bolt together. You have to reach underneath and then shuffle the pieces back and forth to push the bolt through. Sometimes we use awls or worn out screwdrivers to line up the holes. They don't do much quality control on the production line. It shows when we're doing an installation. Rapid and Buckhorn are the worst. We get a job from Interlake, it's a walk in the park. They manufacture beautiful rack. It goes together so fast you don't even have to pound on it. This other shit, we wear out hammers beating it in place. I'm on my third one. I don't know how many screwdrivers I've shattered pounding on the handle. I gave up counting. I just go to Sears and exchange it for another one.

We're working up high now, right beneath the air conditioners. It's really cold here with the air blowing around. The chill goes right through to my spine. I can feel my toes get numb and when that happens I have to step out and warm up. If you can't feel your feet, you don't know what you're standing on. Kenny stays inside and keeps bolting together grating. When I get back he has one side completely finished and we discuss what's next. I stay on one side to Tec screw grating in place and Kenny goes to the other air conditioner to start bolting up that grating. Duane hands it to him and climbs up to help. They get it bolted really fast. I'm fighting this goddamn cheap Tec driver of Carlo's. He's kind of dumb sometimes; buys lousy tools that last about two jobs and then he has to buy more. Kenny got so disgusted with him that he bought his own drill. Good tools make a difference.

The gratings down and I've finished Tec screwing one side when I look over just in time to see Kenny drop about seven feet onto the only beam there he could possibly land on. He lands directly on it with both feet. I can't believe it. The pallet he was standing on split and some small barrels dropped to the ground. They're smashed up and you just know whatever's inside is wrecked. I hide then behind some cartons. The old Mexican hat trick; we'll be gone before they find out. Duane's still laughing at Kenny who's bitching because he's stuck. I climb to where he's wedged between a pallet and the wall. We scoot the pallet away and knock off another carton that lands on the floor below. Kenny looks kind of sheep faced. He climbs back up to the grating and we go back to work.

It's not going bad, about two-thirty and I've finished all the Tec screws. Duane's coiling the extension cord and Kenny has gone to get a supervisor to okay the installation. We're standing there looking around for any tools we've left on the ground when Tony comes blasting through the plastic strips and catches Duane across his Achilles tendon. Tony doesn't honk at all. Duane flies forward onto his stomach in the slush and starts rolling around holding his ankle. His eyes are already full of tears and he's got blood filling his sock. Kenny comes back with the supervisor and we carry Duane outside into the sunshine. I get him propped up under his other leg and Kenny holds his back. Tony stands there watching. I try to unlace his shoe but he's in too much pain to stand it. The supervisor goes to call the hospital and Tony brings around his truck. We load Duane into the bed and start for the hospital. Duane's about as white as me, and Kenny doesn't look so good, either. He's watching Duane gripping his hand in a man's way. I try to keep the leg elevated and wrap it with my flannel shirt to staunch some of the blood. I'm worried about the bleeding but it seems to have slowed down. Kenny and I are really thinking about something else and you can tell Duane's thinking the same thing but no one wants to say the words, like not saying them will keep it from happening. This bastard Tony's taking his time so I pound on the cab and tell him to hurry up. He drives about the same but at least he runs one yellow light. It takes forever to get there. We pass an Urgent Care clinic and then a Kaiser hospital but he keeps going. Finally we get to a complex with a small hospital on one side and a portable building labeled Clinicia on the other. A doctor and nurse come right out and help us get Duane into a wheelchair. Duane is really pale, now. The doctor takes one look at his foot and sends us across the parking lot to the hospital. They take Duane right away and we sit in the lobby with Tony and fill out forms. It seems that this is the company's designated carrier, so they couldn't stop at any other place. Kenny says if Duane's hurt bad, you might as well rename that company

Williams because he's going to own it by the time they get out of court. Kenny calls Carlo and the first thing he asks is did we get the check. Kenny yells `Jesus Christ' at him and some nurses behind the desk give us a dirty look. He hands me the phone and I talk with Carlo a minute. All he cares about is whose fault it was and do we have a witness. I tell him we'll stop by on the way home and hang up. Kenny talks to the nurse behind the desk and then we walk out and around the corner and get a beer at a gas station food mart. We curse Dantel, then Tony, and then Carlo. None of us has any medical. The only protection we have is suing Carlo if we get racked up. He pays for the emergency room stuff when we get hurt on a job, but still it doesn't seem right. He's driving a new crew cab Ford off the profit from our labor and we get a lousy $250 a week. Kenny says he's been thinking about borrowing some money and going to Coast full-time. It's a good idea, I tell him and mention the college girls he'd meet. He smiles and we both almost forget about Duane's injury.

We drain our beers and go back. Duane's in the waiting room looking black again. He's in a wheelchair and holding some crutches on his lap. The doctor gives him some pills and Tony goes out to the truck and opens up the tailgate. We load Duane and climb in and Tony drives real easy to the plant. The good news is that the Achilles tendon isn't cut. The bad news is the doctor took about ten stitches in the soft tissue and Duane's going to be off his game for a couple of months. He might miss the start of the season. It could've been worse; his part-time job could've cost him a college scholarship. We don't mention it, but you can tell by the way we avoid saying anything. When we finally leave Dantel, we decide to forget Carlo and just go home. No one feels much like hanging around after Duane's close call. I ride home carefully and stay out of the fast lane. At my studio apartment I check the mail, open the bills and watch the news. I have tomorrow off. I can take a ride to the ocean and up along the coast. I'll remember to be careful. The smallest thing can really change your life. I might check out Coast on the way back. If Kenny's going to go, I could do all right there. Maybe I could meet a nice girl who likes motorcycles and guys with glasses. Who knows?

The Last Day

The air is different on the last day, and so you know it. Not like rain, when truly something in the air is missing and you can taste the decrease of inches in pressure at the back of your throat; more like missing the punch line or coming in during the last act or talking intimately of old friends with someone whose name you can't remember. Something immediate is inaccessible. You sense that people look at you oddly and greet you with halfhearted enthusiasm like disdain or polite disgust. Your walk seems strained, forced not natural as though you must concentrate on each movement, lifting either leg, exacting conscious execution of articulation, tensor, flexor and rhythm; and this makes you uneasy. So on the last day, you know it.

Sometimes there is a buildup, a leading-up-to that is there between you and your boss and coagulates like good Béchamel when just enough milk has been cooked off or very, very bad gravy. Everyone can see it; of interest only is the manner in which you see it and, this part is important, the manner in which you act.

It is best not to be spiteful or to try to be cunning. Accept the inevitability and make of it your celebration. What more could possibly go wrong? What transgression could you commit which is not rendered moot by acquiescence? Look them in the eye, size up the sons of bitches and tell yourself how lucky you are to get out when you can. Repeat: `This place would have killed me' seven times or until you believe it, whichever comes first. Take a long morning break, fie on productivity, dawdle over a cinnamon roll or make a second trip to the lunchroom for another cup of coffee. Load your desk with supplies, especially things that you might need at home, and then go to lunch early. Eat well but don't drink; no, don't drink. In affairs of dismissal no sense should be waning.

I'll tell you a story. I'll tell you the truth. Maybe not all of the truth but some of the truth all of the time. You decide. There is a part here for everyone; a supervisor, a worker, an assistant with long hair: two disgruntled women you need to like you complaining nonstop of boyfriends or men, and a wannabe actor always performing. That is some

of the truth all of the time. But it really doesn't matter. The
story does not know the difference. It accepts the telling the
way it is told and judges the teller no better or worse. Stories
can do that: like a dog or some grandmothers or a rare friend.
We all need a good story to tell or that kind of love.

Because people are crazy and they want someone to
hate you must go to work and learn how to endure. It should
be a night school course or seminar in which you are trained
like a dog in resignation, sufferance and silent desperation.
You enroll through the mail and meet weekly at a community
college classroom and hope there will be some attractive
woman who finds you irresistibly deep and takes you home
to rub your neck and pour you tea and warm you in her bed.
No such woman appears, but you go to work each day
anyway, because you are newly a dog and dogs know
endurance and endurance is the thing most important to
know in the world. But you already knew that.

The last day often begins like a story: Once upon a
time in the West there was a man . . . . It is like the first day,
really. That same creeping confusion distorts all you hear and
there is that churning in the stomach as if anticipating
calamity. It was this way for me before I learned how much
to care. I answered solicitations, followed leads, expanded my
horizon. Then a phone call, the first interview, and 'we'll call
you.' I waited one week, two weeks, talked myself through
and out of rejection: `I didn't really want that job - a better

offer will come along.' A second interview was arranged. I was confident and calm. With just the right amount of supplication and earnestness, I sold myself cheaply. Two weeks and then into the third, another interview, an offer and acceptance. I marveled at how easily it was accomplished. The first day I was fingerprinted, briefed, given reams of background forms to complete and issued a confidential clearance. I was shown my office and set to work. With celerity and enthusiasm I produced complete redacted copy in hours. My supervisor was impressed, rumors ran rampant, two senior editors commented on my efficacy. I lunched with a coed from Santa Barbara in a tight blouse. Everyone wanted to meet me. I felt liked.

At the end of the second week the office secretary delivered my paycheck. At home I fingered the envelope and dreamed dreams of solvency. It was good.

The secret is that no one ever tells you it will be unimportant. It will be negligible; coffee, communal secretary, per diem for off-site work. It becomes routine. I worked hard, trusted in the corporation, was assured of advancement, bonuses and time off. I learned my job and stayed within my station. I became competent; I became confident. Six months passed. I became a fixture. People asked questions of me. The coed and I were an item. Regular pay, her onsite company (I quickly surpassed her corporate proficiency), lunches with the boss, nights alone with my ingénue. Plans could be laid and she made them. I was handed greater responsibility. I worked diligently and was a success. I learned how to drink at lunch. I gained self-assurance. I became inflexible.

I should have seen it, there is always a sign: "And now presenting . . . ." My boss brought in another, the wannabe actor, mercilessly performing, prancing and affecting. The Jaguar he used to own, the productions on- and off-Broadway in which he had starred, the innumerable sexual conquests and his inexorable virility: "I just wear women out. They can't stay with me for a whole night." I suffered him graciously and affected comradeship. He was the new kid.

And the disgruntled women's man hater bitching over their inability to find reciprocal companionship when all they wanted to find were diversions from hating themselves: They began to hate me. The secretary ignored me and my colleagues no longer asked me questions. My ingénue became distant. I became inconsequential.

So when you walk through the door on the last day and your colleagues appear no longer human but more accurately resemble rodents, nonentities or fodder, you know it. Although the story does not end here.

You walk out the door. It is beautiful, hot and clear and you never return. You will keep hating them for three days and him forever. `If I ever meet him on the street,' you think, `I'll kick his ass. No one can do that to me, no one.' But you know that you'll never meet him on the street and this is all right, too. For no matter how much you hate, he has taught you endurance. And endurance is the most important thing to know in life. That is all the truth.

No wait, there is another part. This is like an epilogue that wants to be a prologue or an induction: The night before the last day you do not sleep well. You are bothered with recurrent indigestion and flatulence and loose stools. In the morning concerns of health are foremost in your mind and carefully you lie, evaluating each body part, in anticipation of pain. When you find nothing identifiably wrong, you move gingerly about your matutinal ablutions and forego coffee.

The day after the last day you feel better than fine.

Running With Raymond

Ray can really get on my nerves. There is nothing of malice or willful iniquity to his actions. He is my friend and he is who he is; a natural born athlete. As we enter the parking lot at the end of our run, he'll elevate his pace, thrust his compact torso forward and begin pumping his arms like a bird flapping its wings for flight. I match him, caught up in the moment, and try to stay by his side. I forget about my deliberate tempo, oblivious to the steady cadence chirping from my runner's wristwatch, and I race. After half-a-minute, my breathing deepens and my chest becomes a cavern of oxygen debt. Ray surges ahead, arms pumping, and before I know it he is a full two-strides in the lead. I am running as fast as I can, willing myself to catch him as we race the remaining distance to the locker room. Ray always has to beat me. We've run together off and on since we met during new-hire orientation two years ago, but regardless of how hard I train or how far we run, I've never, ever beaten Ray. It's making me crazy.

Where I am tall and rangy, Ray is close coupled, compact and taut of muscle like a good quarter horse: A down-sized Samson, easy going, and always quick with a smile. He wears wrap-a-round sunglasses and tosses his tawny, shoulder length mane (really, that is the only way to describe his hair) as he runs. In our department, he gathers his hair together and affects a ponytail that he tucks into the collar of his button down shirt. As we run, he talks about his children and his wife whom he married when she was sixteen and already pregnant with their first child. He tells me about his upbringing in an Inland Empire desert town, dropping out of high school one year before graduation, his minor infractions and many brushes with the law. Claims the Air Force saved his life. Says he'd probably be in jail if he hadn't enlisted: A good looking wife, two children and a great job all as the result of four year's service proffered by a presiding judge in lieu of serving jail time. He was smart enough to take advantage of the training the Air Force provided. He never saw any action.

Across the parking lot from the main building, the company maintains a recreation facility comprising basketball courts, softball fields with a fitness path, and locker rooms with showers. Each day during lunchtime, regulars assemble to exercise. Most of the runners chose to leave the plant property for either the bike trail along the flood control channel or various routes through the surrounding neighborhoods. Ray prefers running the neighborhood, navigating quiet streets and along back alleys or following the access road adjacent the railroad tracks. I like the flood control channel about half-a-mile from the locker room. There are some shallow, holding ponds next to the channel, ample low foliage, and two enormous sycamores in which a pair of Red-tailed hawks roost. In October, migrating Canadian snow geese along the Pacific Flyway stop at the holding ponds and stay for weeks. Near an impassable iron bridge that crosses the flood control channel is a pair of burrowing owls of which I have become quite fond. On a run last year, I brought along my Audubon bird book and stopped to identify the owls. Ray ran on; he said that he wasn't interested in owls.

When I run, I wear the highest quality training shoes, lightweight nylon shorts and a mesh jersey. To cover my balding pate on these sunny days, I wear the cap that I wore in my first marathon. My running technique is studied, efficient, and something of which I am rather proud. I run with a practiced and disciplined gait, properly erect, upper body leaning forward eleven degrees off perpendicular, focusing on a determined push and silent transfer of energy from heel strike to ball of foot. I take time before and after to thoroughly stretch the major muscle groups. I like to visualize every muscle movement while I stretch, imagining how it must look as the ligaments and tendons fill with blood. I always warm up with a few simple exercises according to the recommendations in my running magazines. I discuss with Ray what I have read each month, though like the owls, he isn't really interested. I always give him my old issues.

When Ray runs, he tends to slap his feet at the ground, lean much too far forward and extend his neck. He dresses in either cut-off jeans or a faded pair of swim trunks. Even on the coolest days he never wears a shirt. I always give Ray my old running shoes. The midsoles compact and they lose their ability to absorb shock. It is recommended you replace your shoes every three hundred miles. Ray is still running in the first pair that I gave him. I've never seen him wear any of the others.

Today, it's Ray choice and he wants to run the neighborhood. He does a few, jerky squats in his cut-off jeans while I sit and stretch. I don't like the route. We run in a large loop around the plant, crossing out of one city limit and into another along the way. I don't think it is such a good idea to run along streets or in traffic. There are some interesting sights but I can never give myself over to the running. In the back of my mind I imagine drive-by shootings, gang initiations and anonymous drunks behind the wheel: I hear a car slow on our left, the muzzle of a civilian assault rifle evident in the side window, the rounds coming one after another dusting the ground ahead of us as we run into the fusillade. I look up and an ancient Buick driven by an ancient blue-haired lady comes abreast. I can hear country western music through her open window. We follow to strains of Hank Williams singing Your Cheating Heart as the Buick lumbers past.

Ray is telling me about a vacancy in the computer lab for a senior analyst. I already know about it. I read the posting on the company intranet, talked with human resources this very morning and learned it required a four-year college degree and experience. Human resources would not tell me just when the position would come available. Sometimes they never do come available and are posted by managers as protection against department downsizing. The posting will appear month after month before the position is finally closed. Or the position is advertised to fulfill a 'Government Fair Practices' requirement even though a pre-selected candidate has been assured of the job. It's what I've been waiting for and I intend to apply. With my four-year college degree and good performance reviews, I should have a better than average shot. It would be a smart career move for me, something I need, taking me from my dead-end job to a department with some visibility and opportunity for advancement. At the very least it would represent some professional progress, provide a change in environment and offer increased monetary compensation.

Ray pushes ahead, pumping his arms and twisting backward to talk. He is smiling and saying that he knows the manager who runs the computer lab and as it turns out, he was his master sergeant in the service. At first, I don't get it. Ray has picked up the pace as we leave the city limit and enter an unincorporated area. The trash is different, so you can tell. Pickup is not paid for by city taxes. Paper and Styrofoam line the gutter. Broken down cars absent wheels, hoods, and motors perch on concrete blocks in driveways. Discarded appliances, shattered plastic children's toys, miscellaneous lengths of lumber and stacked tires occupy side yards. A dilapidated RV, with an orange extension cord snaking under the garage door, is parked on the bare, brown yard in front of one house. Ray says that he met with the manager this morning. Ray says that he's been assured that he's getting the job. He laughs and says it's as good as his. The words explode in my head in a gaseous cloud of comic book astonishment and I slow down, stop and watch as he runs farther and farther away. As Ray grows smaller my anger grows bigger. I can feel my face getting red and hot and can hear Ray yelling for me in the distance. I turn around and pick up my pace, my brain a twisted train wreck of enraged carnage high balling for the locker room. I forego stretching and shed my clothes on the floor near my locker.

I am a long time in the shower. My face burns in the cold spray and my temples pound. I tell myself that I should be happy for Ray; I should congratulate him. But what I want to do is hurt Ray, attack him with unprecedented malevolence and ferocity, drop him to his knees with a kick to the groin and take this penknife on my key chain and slash at his pacific smile. Over in a jiffy and clearly a merciful act, no jury in the land would convict me. I am intoxicated by the immediacy of the concept. The very image of severed flesh, blood spattering my trousers, shoes, parked cars; the horror in Ray's face as he searches for me through wrecked, tearing eyes. It makes me smile with guilty pleasure as I leave the locker room. Across the parking lot, I can see Ray at his car putting his running gear into the trunk. He smiles and waves, and I can't help myself but wave back, and then he jogs towards the main building. I stuff my hands in my pockets and finger my key chain against my thigh. The penknife nestles between thumb and index finger and I smile, too. Maybe some collateral mischief is in order, a single valve stem, just one tire, that's all. Nothing that a well-connected guy about to get an undeserved promotion and a good-looking wife and a nice family couldn't address at the end of a long day. What's one tire, anyway? An offhand rebuke in the middle of a polite conversation? A necessary reality check on a sunny day? Ahead is Ray's car and the penknife is open and poised in my palm. Ray is my friend, but I don't think that I can run with him anymore.

Growers

On a bank above a small creek we have built a campfire large enough to warm three men at the perimeter. Occasionally someone stands, turns their back to the heat and then sits in the low chairs Phil has thought to provide. Coyotes howl, firewood cracks and pops; small game stalk a chary circumference just beyond the purlieus of dancing light. Out of sight a furious nocturnal commotion tears at the underbrush. Phil laughs, shows his crooked teeth and licks his moustaches; Robbie lights a cigarette. A pint of Old Crow warmed in transit by four hands comes my way.

"Still drinking the good stuff?"

"I ain't never changed," Robbie says proudly and tilts the bottle arm's length above his mouth.

"Still crazy after all these years, is what he means,"

Phil says.

"Same steam same steam," Robbie answers and nods a crooked smile.

"I got some anti-freeze in the truck over there," Phil says and points toward the pickup."

"It is tempting," Robbie says.

I laugh and shake my head.

"You're still crazy," I say.

"I'm not alone," Robbie answers. "Difference is, I'm on the other side of the switch."

Phil and Robbie picked me up at the regional airport this morning. We stopped in Bethel, a dying Central Valley town, where I bought a plaid hat with ear flaps, brown canvas jacket, wool socks and tall, leather boots. In an instant I became a different person, a returning pack member of my college friends, no longer the city outsider but an integral part of the rural landscape. I wore my hat far back on my head and strutted my eight-inch leather boots. I hefted a bolt-action .308 Savage in my soft, city hands. My flight leaves Sunday night and I've already gotten carried away. I'm not certain what I'll do with the back-woods paraphernalia I've already purchased. There aren't many occasions for a corporate number cruncher to wear country motley in a boardroom. I'll probably leave everything with Phil until the next time we go camping, but I think I'll keep the hat. Some unseasonably cool morning, with the brim folded in two, I'll tuck it into the back pocket of my pinstripe trousers and take it to the office. I can put it on at lunch while I sit in the courtyard and reflect on the tragic triviality of my professional life. That would be something.

"Man, look at the stars. Fantastic."

We murmur in agreement.

"Don't get out here enough," Phil says. He goes to the tent and returns with planisphere and miniature flashlight.

"You're a sissy-man, now," Robbie says. "That marriage got you pussy-whipped and soft."

Phil looks at him coolly. "Maybe we can see Halley's," he says to me.

"Mountain man wouldn't need no chart," Robbie says.

Phil shines his miniature flashlight in Robbie's eyes and grabs for the bottle. Robbie shrugs his shoulders.

"Mountain man wouldn't," he mumbles.

*   *   *

It is difficult to make friends when you've left the nucleus of common aspiration. I met these two because my high school adviser recommended a rural college in Northern California with an experimental freshman curriculum that overlooked truancy, a marginal SAT and provided a minimal living stipend for low-income applicants. Phil was working at a local restaurant where I found a part time job cooking. He had got into trouble in high school but his credits were sufficient to let him graduate early at which point he packed his belongings and girlfriend into a Pennsylvania rust-belt beater, raised his middle finger to the past and moved to California. He seemed already to be an adult when I met him, while I was just leaving adolescence, my hometown for the first time, and the mother who had raised me alone.

I knew little about restaurant work and he took me under his wing and showed me the ropes: How to cook, how to behave as an employee, how to work with a level of professionalism I'd ignored in my high school summer jobs. He wanted to do something in Forestry so that he could live in the mountains. I didn't know what I wanted to do but we were both in college, slogging our way through required coursework one semester at a time and living paycheck to paycheck; we had that much in common. After a while, as I learned my way around a commercial kitchen and lost some of my city affectation, we became friends. We worked together on the evening shift, attended classes during the day and lived in a falling-down all but forgotten rental farmhouse at the edge of a black walnut orchard on the outside of town. Our disposable income went for beer, groceries when we couldn't steal enough food from the restaurant, and trying to get laid.

Then Robbie joined us. We met him shooting pool

at a college bar where he held one table the entire night. He showed up the next afternoon at the farmhouse with a case of beer and a deck of cards. We played Hearts and he beat me out of eleven dollars. He said he'd been busted for possession twice but never convicted and that was okay because he was still crazy. He rode a battered Yamaha and pulled a wheel stand without any headlights all the way down the dark road when he left. He started hanging around more and more and calling us the Musketeers. One afternoon, he arrived with a duffle bag across the tank of his motorcycle and moved in. He slept in a sleeping bag on a wooden cot in the unheated screen porch all year round. Robbie was alone in the world, turned out of an Oakland orphanage when he turned 18, and he needed a place to be. Phil, like me, had a mother two thousand miles away in the past. We formed our own family out of mutual need and lived together in that rental farmhouse for five years. Through chance and circumstance, different as we were, we had met and I looked up to both of them. They each had checkered histories ingloriously propelling them into manhood and, though by comparison, my past seemed uninspired, they were my friends. Those two were already Musketeers, and I aspired to be the third.

Phil and I finished school and I think as a result of our encouragement, Robbie completed a program that got him a job in the penal system at the prison outside of town.

He worked his way up the organizational ladder and now oversees executions. I moved back to Los Angeles to begin my career in business and Phil married a local girl, landed a job with the Department of the Interior, and bought a house not far from where we'd rented. Though we are geographically and professionally separate, I still consider these two my friends and stay in contact with holiday greetings, postcards when I vacation, phone calls when I'm feeling especially lonesome. Having spent so much of ourselves together, there isn't much left for words. Our conversations are limited to enquiries of health and employment or recent acquisitions. Phil likes to camp and explore; he still fancies himself a mountain man. Robbie's a gambler and regularly plays cards in Reno or Tahoe always hoping for the big score. I lose a lot of hours at the office and fill free time upgrading my audio equipment; I have a pair of Dynaco tube-state amps that are better than you would find in most recording studios, and English speakers in laminated concrete cabinets that weigh more than 50 lbs. I don't know if Robbie does drugs anymore.

"How's Candy?" I ask Phil.

"Working too much, as usual."

Phil's voice trails off inviting remark. Robbie doesn't seem to notice.

"Still thinking about starting a family?" I ask.

Phil clears his throat and shakes his head. Robbie

laughs a little, as though I've made a good joke.

"Fucking-Eh."

We sit and listen to the crackling of the fire. Around comes the bottle, and then beer follows. Phil lights a cigarette off Robbie's and exhales toward his face.

"You know, for a married guy," Robbie says, "This is a weekend without your woman."

He pauses long enough to hold our attention and to drag on his cigarette.

"But for single guys," he says, and looks at me, "this is another weekend without a woman."

"Fucking-Eh."

We laugh, mumble and take turns shaking our heads. Phil tosses a few sticks onto the coals and we quietly watch them burn. After a while, he stands and stretches.

"I'm hitting it," he says. "See you assholes in the morning."

*   *   *

Phil works with his hands. They wear the weathering of constant exposure. If there's a problem, he confronts it head on. You can see it in his economical movement and the way that he accomplishes tasks even while relaxing. Every trip he makes to the truck, he carries something each way. He planned the camping trip, organized equipment, consulted his collection of topographical maps and identified all the thermal springs in the area. Our campsite is 200 yards from a hot spring the size of a washtub. When we arrived, the first thing he did was to fetch a pail of heated water. He held it up, waved his callused hand in the steam rising from the surface, bowed dramatically and poured it onto the bushes. It is these eccentricities of his that are so endearing.

"Had enough?" Robbie asks. We finish our beers and head for the tent. I situate myself so that I can see the night sky through the gauze netting. Robbie starts snoring almost immediately. I lie and watch the fire burn down until it is just a chalky glow of dying embers.

*   *   *

When I wake, Phil is stoking the campfire and brushing his teeth. He points to a bucket of water and I retrieve soap and towel. The water is warm and, as I look up in surprise, Phil nods and smiles. He lights a cigarette and by the time I've finished washing there are three enamelware mugs next to the coffee pot. We place our chairs close to the fire ring waiting for the coffee to brew.

Overhead, the morning sky is gray and threatening. Clouds scud and pack, the sun becomes blackened and almost instantly the temperature drops. The aroma of pines and sage, something I don't get to smell in the city, fills the air. It reminds me of the differences in the lives we live. I am in the mountains and this is Phil's world. Robbie emerges from the tent with his crooked smile. He sits by the fire, takes a cigarette from Phil's pack and pours coffee. He looks up at the sky.

"Wonderful morning. Love this kind of weather," he says and scratches at his beard.

Phil has topo maps spread in his lap. I wonder what time it is, think about getting my wristwatch, stand up, and sit down as I change my mind. Time doesn't really matter when you're camping.

"What say to some breakfast, Musketeers?"

Phil pokes at the fire and situates a grill to accommodate a fry pan. In a matter of minutes we are eating bacon and fried eggs. We drink the last of the coffee and collect our gear as Phil spreads the fire coals. Robbie carries his government issue .38 Special holstered in the middle of his back and wears a camouflaged hunting cap. Phil has a rucksack with beer, powerful field binoculars, spiral notebook and an old, long barreled .32 that belonged to his father. I have my Swiss army knife and a monocular around my neck that I take when I sightsee. We are checking Phil's maps when a man and woman pass on the creek trail below our camp. They are both slight in build, mid-twenties, furtive. She is dressed in jeans and war surplus military jacket. He wears a worn sweatshirt, dark khaki pants, and a knit cap covering most of his head. Each has a lightly loaded duffle bag over their shoulder and carries a gallon jug of water in each hand. The man quickly glances up but the woman keeps her eyes to the ground as they pass.

"Growers or middlemen?" Robbie asks.

"Definitely growers," Phil says. "Ferrying supplies. Probably working upriver somewhere weekend hikers don't go."

"What do we do?" I ask.

"We could follow 'em," Robbie says.

"Purloin the spoils of their labor," Phil says with a broad smile. "That could be profitable."

Robbie nods his head, his smile more psychotic this time than crooked, and flicks his cigarette into the dying coals.

"It's a take no prisoners proposition," he says, and scratches his beard. "No prisoners."

"Fucking-Eh," I say and they both look at me as if I've committed a faux pas. I look at Phil and then Robbie.

"Fucking-Eh it is," Robbie finally says and we all laugh.

The sky is growing darker and the air tastes like rain. I can feel the change in barometric pressure, as if a door just opened in a closed room; something seems very different.

We set out along a well-worn path that descends to the creek, continue for about a mile, and then stop at the remains of a bridge. The bridge comprises stone piers, filled with river rock wrapped in wire fencing, and rotted wooden planks. It seems less than safe. Time and weather have worked at the foundation, dropping one side lower than the other so that we walk downhill as we cross. Phil says there used to be a chromium mine above us. He has a genuine curiosity about these mountains and one day he'll be the only one left who has recorded what remains of the Central Valley's West Side precious metal's craze. He comes over with his map.

"You ready to push on? The mine's about two miles ahead, up this trail."

We begin to hike. First a gentle, slight angle, then the trail becomes much steeper. It takes all my concentration to step over fallen trees, rocks big as footballs, around car-sized boulders. As I struggle along behind Robbie, I listen to my pounding heart, songbirds, and the gusting wind in the trees as the sky grows darker. The new boots rub against my anklebone causing me to wince and adjust my step.

The mine is located on one peak of a ridge saddle. There are warning signs posted on chain strung between posts blocking the entrance. Fire blackened lumber is strewn about: half-a-dozen two by fours and charred planks, some lengths of cable, a coil of rusted chain. I pick up a square, hand forged nail from the debris. Phil has walked out of sight and calls. We join him and see another peak not twenty feet below. A path is worn to an outhouse abutting a drop-off. It is green plastic, in good repair, with a dull white roof. I can hear the door rattle in the wind from where I stand.

Phil goes first while Robbie gets beers and sits down along the ridge. The air is colder, the wind buffeting us in surges, and to the East storm clouds blanking out the sun roll toward us. I loosen my new boots and adjust my sock. I can already taste the rain.

"It's only a matter of time before all hell breaks loose," Robbie says and raises his beer toward the sky. "How's work in the big city?"

I lean next to him against a boulder the size of a Volkswagen.

"It's all right. Maybe a promotion for me at the end of the year. And a bonus. How about you?"

Robbie drinks at his beer and shakes his head.

"Still cleaning up God's mess," he says. "One maggot at a time."

"Who's next?" Phil calls as he comes toward us. "Man, it's beautiful, sitting there, the door wide open and those thunderheads moving in. Just you and your thoughts in the plastic confessional."

I take my turn and Phil is right. The storm clouds spilling over the ridge filling the valley below is spectacular to see. I finish my business, return to the boulder and Robbie takes my place. Phil and I drink our beers and watch the storm clouds churn. The sun is hidden now behind a dense black carpet creeping up the slope. Robbie joins us, cigarette in his mouth, and Phil repacks his rucksack and stands.

"Let's follow this trail along the ravine. We'll come out about a mile down stream from the camp. We can cross the creek somewhere and hike back up from there. Maybe we can beat the storm. You guys ready?"

"Fucking-Eh."

The descent is easy along a well-established path that drops quickly beneath the ridge saddle. No one says much. I follow Phil and Robbie follows me. Near the bottom of the ravine we lose the path and have to break trail, ducking beneath broken tree limbs and climbing around boulders. We stop at a small clearing with a plastic pipe sticking out of a weeping fissure in the rocky slope and three, five-gallon buckets sitting in a shallow pool of water. A hollow cave opening littered with candy wrappers is partially hidden behind stacked tree branches. Nearby come two male voices. Phil motions to me and then steps off the trail. I watch and then follow Robbie to the far side of the clearing. We stand together as two men appear from below. One is the man in the knit cap; the other is a very dark-skinned man wearing knee high boots, a blue quilted vest and carrying a shotgun. His hair is a mat of kinky bristles exploding outward in different lengths and his face is filthy. He looks like a feral alley cat long accustomed to fending for itself. They both stop as they see us. Nobody speaks; nobody moves. The shotgun stays at the feral man's side, the other man stands behind him and below. Robbie is the first to step forward and speak.

"Seems we got off the trail. We must be lost."

Silence folds over both groups. Robbie has moved to the right an arm's length away from me with his hand behind his back on his holster. I am watching the eyes of the feral man. They gleam black, wild and without depth or understanding, darting from one face to another. The shotgun is motionless, barrel angled toward the ground near our feet. The silence is broken by the wind and a light rain begins to fall. The man in the knit cap speaks.

"You must be lost brother. Could it be you're lost, brother? Are you lost?"

Something is not right. From one face to another the feral man's wild eyes jump. The wind blows and an odor part earth, urine and human stench assaults my nose. I watch as the feral man grips the shotgun with his other hand and his eyes open wide. Like a scene from a Hollywood movie, I imagine it; the shotgun rising, the explosive blast, the scramble of bodies and the ensuing bloodshed. The man in the knit cap is smiling as the sky bursts open and drops of driving rain pound like machine gun shots around us. They splash in tiny craters and ricochet around our feet. Lightning cracks and I jump out of my skin, catching myself and looking at the others looking at me. This is it, I think. This is the kind of thing you read about in the newspaper. 'Three dead bodies found in local mountains; no witnesses.' People say that they can see their own accidents as they happen and still they don't believe what they see. Phil steps out from the brush behind the man in the knit cap.

"Nobody wants any trouble," he says.

Both men freeze and the man in the knit cap slowly turns his head to look. The feral man starts fidgeting, jerking his head from one person to another, his gleaming black eyes narrowed now, mouth open as if to speak, stained fingers flexing on the stock of the shotgun as he looks expectantly at the man in the knit cap. Then he clamps his jaw and I can almost see the thought form in his feral brain. I'm paralyzed, my heartbeat ringing in my head and a desperate scream builds low in my chest like a swelling crescendo of disbelief fighting upward for release. He reaches for the shotgun slide with his other hand and pumps a shell into the chamber. Before the barrel can rise, Phil takes two quick steps toward him and has his .38 Special a foot from the feral man's forehead. The rain drives into my face and I swallow hard to hold back the scream. I stare into the feral man's eyes and they look to the man in the knit cap and then back to Robbie. Robbie smiles his crooked smile. The feral man stares directly at Robbie's smiling face and then looks to the man in the knit cap. The rain splashes soundlessly around us and lightning bolts silently charge the black sky and the only noise I hear is the hammer on the .38 Special as it clicks into cocked position. Phil steps closer to the man in the knit cap and levels his revolver at his back. The man turns to face him, looks down at the revolver and then stares into Phil's eyes for what seems a long time. All at once the storm returns and roars around me, whipping the underbrush against my shins and pelting my face with raindrops.

"Ya mut b' los'," the feral man says and bares a mouthful of stained, broken teeth. The shotgun is rigid in one hand, index finger laced around the trigger. Phil cautiously circles the two men, walking backward. His eyes are fixed on the man in the knit cap, the revolver pointing at his chest.

"Make a decision," he says and raises the revolver higher. "Make it now."

The man in the wool cap nods at the feral man and the shotgun slowly lowers to his side. Robbie steps away, keeping the .38 Special aimed on target and stops a few yards to the side of Phil.

"The trail must be back here," Phil says. The rain blows into my face and I blink it out of my eyes. Another crack of lightning behind us shakes the ground but not one of us moves. We stand in the small clearing, weapons raised, facing the others.

"We're just on a one time trip," Phil says, talking

pointedly at the man in the knit cap.

He smiles unusually white teeth. It is a perfect smile, exhibiting professional orthodontia and regular hygiene. We start walking backwards, eyes fixed on the two men, watching the shotgun, bumping into each other as we negotiate the wet ground. The rain has slacked as lightning arcs across the sky to the West. Phil stops walking and Robbie and I hike through the overgrowth, back the way we'd come, for twenty yards or so, out of sight. Robbie immediately begins backtracking our route. He disappears off trail and I stand straining to see through the overgrowth. For some reason it occurs to me that these, my oldest friends, are going after the growers. I listen for the shots and Phil strides around the corner and lifts his finger to his lips. Rain splashes from his hand onto his face and he wipes at his cheeks with his sleeve.

"Keep moving, don't talk."

We hurry up the incline we'd descended and stop at a point where we can see the opening below. My heart is still racing but I am surprisingly calm. The growers are nowhere to be seen.

"Where's Robbie?" I ask.

Phil shakes his head. The long barrel revolver is still in his hand pointed at the ground. The rain falls so lightly it's just a mist and we walk a little farther, stop, and huddle beneath the low branches of a pine. Lightning flashes and backlights the gray clouds, and a crash of thunder echoes off the mountains. Its rumble is mixed with a single report and we both jerk downward ducking our heads for cover. Phil steps from beneath the tree branches and starts down the trail. He takes a few steps and stops, revolver loose at his side, as Robbie brushes past him and then past me. We follow for a hundred yards before Phil grabs at Robbie's sleeve. Robbie stops, looks at Phil, then me, then past my head toward the ridge saddle.

"Best break camp soon as we get back," he says.

He turns but Phil has a good hold of his sleeve and stops his progress. He stares at Robbie and Robbie spreads his arms as if asking for forgiveness. It is almost peaceful, the wind abated as the storm moves West, silent gray moisture like Tule fog drifting past and coloring the air. A shaft of sunlight slips through the fog and cuts across the far bank of the ravine.

Robbie crosses his arms and looks directly at me.

"We're in this together, Musketeers," he says.

He turns and begins hiking. We follow single file behind Robbie for half a mile until Phil finds where we lost the trail and takes the lead. The wind blows lightly and dries the rain from my cheeks. Sunlight pierces thinning clouds and dapples the overgrowth with a preternatural glow along the creek bank. The campsite above the river is in view. We arrive, collapse the tents with everything inside and put them in the truck bed. The cook gear goes into its box and is stacked along with the chairs on top of the tents to hold them in place. I watch Robbie, cigarette in his mouth, kicking the ring of stones from around the fire pit. We drive down the road and around the first bend Phil slows next to a rusted, white cargo van. Robbie climbs out, looks into the rear glass and nods at Phil. I climb out, too, from the back seat, and stand next to him. Inside the van are empty five gallon buckets, folded blankets and bulging, lumpy plastic trash bags. Robbie looks at me and I know what to do. I take my Swiss Army knife from my pocket, open the short blade and saw at the valve stem of the front tire. Air rushes out and the van settles onto the wheel rim. Robbie nods again and returns to the truck. I walk to the rear tire, squat down, and look at Robbie. He shakes his head and climbs into the back seat as Phil gives me a look and revs the truck motor. I stare at the van, the others, and the waning storm rolling toward the horizon. I pocket my knife and climb into the truck. Lightning flashes to the West but the thunder is a long time coming. As we drive down the mountain, I watch the receding storm as Phil and Robbie smoke cigarettes. Phil hangs his arm out the side window and Robbie slouches across the rear seat like he's ready to nap. I stare through the windshield as the valley floor grows nearer. There is nothing left to be said.

Christmas Vision

It is the day before Christmas in 1968 and we are driving toward Bellingham. The New York Jets are going to the AFC title game and the talk on the radio is of Joe Namath. My father listens intently and yells at the chrome speaker bezel. I think that he winks at me in the mirror and rolls his eyes. Beneath my Beatles' haircut I wear black, lensless eyeglasses. The rain drizzles against the windshield and my mother takes wadded tissue from her purse and wipes at her nose. It is three days after my tenth birthday and I know what it means to be myopic.

"Some kind of day for tree shopping," my father says. He reaches for the dash, adjusts the knob on the radio and turns on the wipers. They flip across the windshield in parallel, slowing and increasing in speed for no apparent reason. Then the wiper on my father's side slows and I decide to hold my breath until it speeds up. The passenger side wiper continues at regular speed. The slop-slop of the blades sweeping the rain from the windshield separates and becomes slop, slop-slop, slop, slop-slop. I listen carefully and count the sweeps until a complete cycle passes and the two wipers are in sync. I breathe with the rhythm and try to make my heartbeat match the wipers. Then my mother's wiper stops moving so I have to hold my breath again and my mother reaches her hand and points just as my father begins pounding on the windshield and yelling "God-damn-it." My mother says "Now..." the way she always does at my father's outbursts and then "Oh!" The wipers shape up and I can breath again.

"Persuasion," my father says and I think that he winks at me in the rear view mirror. "Every salesman worth his salt yells a little," he says, looking through the rain-smeared windshield. The rain is coming down harder, pounding on the roof and blowing into the open crack at the wind wing. Ahead the traffic has stopped. My father rolls down his side window and pushes his head into the storm. The wiper on my father's side halts completely as the other continues to sweep back and forth so I have to hold my breath again. I can't see anything through the window at all. Everything is fuzzy like usual with my crummy eyes and now even worse with the rain. Beside me my older sister makes

140

her loud, bored sigh and my mother turns in her seat and smiles at her with her mother eyes. I give my sister my mean face and she mouths 'Four Eyes' at me and wags her head.

"We got a wreck up here, Marcia. Some idiot driving with his mind on hold."

"I think it's just someone off to the side, dear," my mother says.

This is my father's expression. To him, everything that goes wrong in the world is because someone has their mind on hold. Government mistakes, dropped passes in the end zone, even traffic accidents could be prevented if people's minds were not on hold. When I forget stuff or do something dumb he asks: "What's wrong with you? You got your mind on hold?" and stares waiting for an answer but I'm just a skinny kid with crummy eyes. I'm smart in school and my mother always tells me that 'A good mind is a blessing' like that's enough. She's just trying to keep me from feeling bad.

"God-damn-it!" my father shouts and pounds his fist against the windshield. Miraculously both wipers begin and sweep in unison. He looks into the rear view mirror and maybe winks. I take a deep breath and pull out my birthday money from my pocket. I have two dollars and twenty-five cents that my mother told me to save for a rainy day.

The traffic inches forward and we follow another station wagon filled with people. Their windows are steamed over but I think some kind of dog is moving around in the back. The station wagon moves ahead and my father guns the Ford, spinning the tires, on the wet street like a teenager. I think he grins at me in the mirror. He is trying to cheer me up in that way of his. He likes to pull pranks at the table, tell a few jokes and kid around with me. I wear my lens-less eyeglasses and imagine what it will be like when I can see all things with corrected vision. Already I have trouble at school with guys who want to pick on me because I am skinny, though my mother calls me slender, now I have the eyeglasses to worry about and the heavy, leather brogues, too. I wear them to fix my feet. I do not like to wear them but my mother tells me when I'm grown I'll be glad that I did. Each year, at the beginning of school, I get new school clothes. That means two pairs of corduroys, button down shirts and always a new pair of brogues. The man at the shoe store knows me and carefully fits each pair with tongue pads and arch supports that will fix my flat feet. While my classmates wear two-tone saddle oxfords, penny loafers or even Converse Smilies, I wear brogues. When the brogues are getting new soles or heels, I get to wear my Rod Taylors with no arch supports. They are like flying for my feet. I can run, jump and float in the air. I leap tall guardrails along the road to school, balance on the high handrail that climbs the steps, and squeak the soles in the hallway as though I were on the gymnasium floor. I feel like I'm one of the regular guys.

Sometimes I swagger a bit, I know, because my mother has cautioned me about acting too big for my britches. The high tops are white and too wide for my skinny feet so I put insoles inside and wear two pairs of socks. I wish I could wear them all the time but usually I have to wear the brogues.

"All right, all right. Move it or park it!" my father yells at the windshield. The station wagon has pulled off at a service station and we creep along close behind a blue sedan. Our car is sticky hot and the windows are fogging even though it is hardly raining now. My mother pulls more tissue from her purse and wipes at the glass, first my father's side, then hers. She reaches back and passes me the wad of tissue. It is soggy and useless. I rub at my side window with the sleeve of my jacket and practice watching out the window in my eyeglasses.

On the weekends, my father and I work around the house. He wakes me early, before my mother or sister are up, and tells me what we are doing that day while we eat cereal together in the kitchen. These are the best times. We usually have to buy parts for something we are repairing, like the station wagon or the washing machine, and sometimes I even figure out what is wrong before my father can. Then he tells me I'm smart just like he is and I like that. We always stop at the donut shop on our way to get supplies. I get a maple bar and grape juice and my father always puts his extra change in the March of Dimes box even if it's almost a dollar then says hello in his big voice to all the guys in the donut shop, shouting across the room or telling a joke as he spills sugar into his coffee cup and on the counter. Sometimes the guys say hello to me and tell me I look just like my father which makes me feel good. They always say goodbye like they know us when we leave.

We approach a car on the other side of the road with a tree tied to the roof. The back end has slid into the ditch and the owner has one foot on the rear bumper looking at the submerged wheel. He holds a newspaper above his head and balances with his other hand on the trunk. All at once he loses his footing and one leg shoots into the air and he drops in a sitting position onto the muddy embankment. My sister lets out a shriek and giggles behind her hand. My mother giggles some, too, and then holds a tissue to her mouth.

"That poor man," she says still giggling while I hear my father say 'Idiot' under his breath.

"He has a white tree. Let's get a white tree this year," my sister cries.

"No white tree," my father says and gives her the eye in the rear view mirror, I think. "It's not your choice, anyway."

"But I want one. I want one, anyway," my sister says.

"That's enough," says my father and my mother turns around before she can say anything and points her finger and then smiles.

"Don't argue with your father."

My sister is in seventh grade this year and says that she doesn't believe in Christmas, anymore. I don't believe in the Santa Claus stuff, but Christmas is okay. I like the gifts. We each get one big present and usually two little ones. And of course now I'm getting the eyeglasses but they don't count as a present because I need them. I still get A's in school but I can't read the black board or the clock. My sister crosses her arms, gets her pouty look, mouths 'Four Eyes' at me and kicks at the back of the front seat.

"Hey!" my father yells and tries to look mad in the mirror and then winks at me, I think. He turns up the radio and Joe Namath is talking about the upcoming game.

"Now that's confidence!" He says.

My mother shakes her head and clicks her tongue. The Christmas tree lot is ahead and we pull off and park a distance from the sales hut. The rain has stopped but there are still puddles. Everyone piles out of the car and the Christmas tree smell and the rain mix together and I can't feel bad even if I have flat feet and crummy eyes and will have to wear eyeglasses for the rest of my life. I go one way searching for our tree and my sister and mother go another. I know just what to look for: a Blue Spruce. Each year we get a different type of tree and this year I got to choose. They aren't really blue but I can't tell colors correctly because I'm colorblind. I just like the idea of someone calling a tree blue

145

when everyone knows they're supposed to be green. My father comes over to me and a tree lot boy approaches. He's wearing knee-high rain boots, a hooded parka and eyeglasses with one thick lens and the other lens colored black. I can't see behind the black lens and he screws up his face and squints like me when he talks so his other eye gets even smaller.

"We want the finest Blue Spruce Christmas tree on the lot," my father says and smiles his big smile.

"We have some over here," the tree lot boy says and starts walking away. My father turns to me and gives me his funny surprised look and then follows. My mother and sister are in the next row and they come over to where we are standing. Everywhere there are beautiful Blue Spruce trees around us and I know just which one. I point to it and my father gives the tree lot boy his inquiring look.

"Is that your best one, son?" he asks in his serious voice.

"I don't know, sir. But I think it's nice," the tree lot boy answers and screws up his face again squinting now even more than I do.

"So do I," I agree and give the tree lot boy my best smile because he has crummy eyes, too.

"I better ask the little lady," my father says. "Marcia, what do you think about this one?"

"It's a little big, don't you think, honey?" my mother

says and then looks at me to see if I'm disappointed.

My father looks at me and says, "Thinking big never hurt anybody," and then pretend punches me in the arm.

"How much is it?" my mother asks the tree lot boy. He gets out a measuring tape and stretches it from the ground beneath his boot to almost the top of the tree but it's over his head. He takes a length of measuring tape and extends it so that it bends above and then he tries to reach up and mark it with his hand at the top of the tree. The measuring tape comes loose at his foot and snaps upward and he has to start over. When he gets the measuring tape extended this time he bobs his head and I can tell that he's having trouble reading the numbers. He twists his head and squints at the tape measure. We stand around waiting and my father is just about to say something when my mother takes his arm and steps forward.

"I think it's just the right one for us," she says in her mother's voice to the tree lot boy. "We'll take it."

The tree lot boy keeps struggling with the measuring tape and my mother gives my father her serious look and a nod of her chin and then he steps up and says "That's got to be a seven footer if I ever saw one, son. Wouldn't you agree?"

"If you say so," he says and the tape measure slips from his hand and falls in the water on the ground. He has to squint to find it in the puddle.

"We'll take it just as it is," my father says and puts his hand on the tree lot boy's shoulder and gives it a smile. The tree lot boy gets out a pad and holds it close to his nose and writes down the tree and size and gives my father the receipt.

"We've got that Ford Country Squire right there," he says. "Let's put it on the roof."

My father and I carry the tree to the car and put it on the roof and the tree lot boy follows us with a big ball of twine. He stands watching us and twists his head while my father and I tie the tree to the roof rack. The rain has started again and my sister and mother sit in the car as my father examines the receipt and pulls a five and two ones from his wallet. Then he stops and looks at the tree lot boy again, smiles, opens the car door and leans across to my mother.

"Marce, I need a ten," he says.

"How much is it?" she asks as she gets out of the car and takes the receipt. "Well, how much?"

My father smiles and shakes his head.

"But it's only...." she says.

"Marce, it's Christmas."

My mother hands the money to my father. The tree lot boy has walked over with the ball of twine to stand out of the rain at the sales hut. He's looking back toward us but is having some trouble finding where we are.

"Look?" I say and point. My father looks at him,

then me and then my mother. I take the ten-dollar bill from him and walk toward the tree lot boy. He is still searching for us, twisting his head and not seeing where we stand by the car. The rain is coming down harder. I walk up to the tree lot boy and hand him the money. He squints at it with his one good eye and than at me. I can tell that he doesn't know what to say.

"Here you go," I say and turn around. My father and mother and are standing next to the car watching me. I remember my rainy day money and pull out my two dollars and twenty-five cents and give it to the tree lot boy.

"Keep the change," I say just like my father would and walk away. When I get to the car my mother is giving me a different look but my father has his big smile. I turn around and the tree lot boy is still standing in the same spot.

"Merry Christmas," I say with my big voice. My father messes my hair and we get into the car. My sister has climbed into the back so I have the entire rear seat for myself.

"That's a very nice thing you did," my mother says and then looks at my father. He starts the car and races the engine. I can see the tree lot boy standing by the sales hut. He watches for us as we pull across the lot and wait to enter traffic. My mother puts her hand on my father's shoulder.

"That poor boy. And with only one eye," she says in her mother's voice.

My father guns the car and shoots across two lanes and merges into traffic. He makes his big smile in the mirror and I know that he gives me a wink.

"It's Christmas time now, kids. Let's get this tree home," he says and turns on the radio.

My mother turns around and sees me with the black eyeglass frames in my hand. She gives me a different look. The radio crackles and the wipers rhythmically swipe back and forth across the windshield without missing a beat. I breathe easy with them and then watch as the tree lot gets fuzzy.

"See that?" my father asks and points at the wipers. "Everything's good at Christmas."

On the way to our house I practice wearing my eyeglasses and think about having good eyes. I forget for a second and reach into my pocket for my two dollars and twenty-five cents birthday money and remember the tree lot boy. I see my reflection in the mirror and give myself the wink. I don't worry any more about my eyeglasses.

Billy's Grade

At the farm I always leaned against the fender and Billy would drive. The hard part was keeping your feet on the differential; as the ruts bumped and jerked the tractor from side to side, I'd hook my boots along the alloy casting and rock with the motion. Sometimes my hands would slip on the smooth steel fender and Billy would reach for me if I were falling. He caught me once and the second time I caught myself. At that he grinned his broken yellow teeth and shook his head.

"We'll teach you yet," he said.

My grandmother was in the kitchen prattling to herself at the sink, and as I sat she put a serving platter of hotcakes in the middle of the table and poured me coffee from a blackened kettle. It was cold that early summer morning. The hoar frost stayed on the ground until noon and in the kitchen grandmother kept a small, wood stove banked against the morning chill. My cousin Michael sat down at the other side of the table. He was visiting, too, and only drank grandmother's coffee with lots of cream and sugar. Each morning complained of a sour stomach and didn't clean his plate.

Billy came in from the barn with a hatchet in one hand. I watched as he poured coffee, reversed a chair, sat and laid his long arms across the back. He slurped at his coffee and smacked his lips and set.

"Just how I like it, hot and black," he said. "I'll need some help with a cow, today. Just one will be enough. The other can tend to grandma."

He watched grandma at the stove and laid the hatchet on the table.

'Give it to me give it to me'.

I thought then that if I could think something hard enough, Billy could hear me. I wanted to be just like him. He encompassed all that I thought was rugged, tough and manly. He rode Rusty, the cutting horse; he cursed, spit and smoked his own hand rolled cigarettes. No one could beat Billy at anything. He was the star high school running back and had been to community college in Portland, for a year, before he came back to run the farm to take the 4H extension course. Everyone knew Billy because he was special. Driving through

Castle Rock people would lean out the windows of their pickups and holler hello as they passed him on the street.

Michael had stopped eating with his fork held between the plate and his mouth. He watched Billy and then looked at me. Billy looked at Michael and then me and I thought as loud as I could. He extended the hatchet to me head first and I grabbed at it, dropping it on the spent, kitchen floor.

"You're it, pardoner. Let's get to it."

My grandmother picked up the hatchet and handed it to Billy.

"He hasn't finished his meal, Billy. You him be."

Billy smiled, drank the last of his coffee and slowly stood up from the chair.

"I'll be getting the tractor."

I waited for grandmother to turn back to the stove and put my last hotcake beneath the top one on the serving platter and shoved the remainder of my breakfast into my mouth.

"I'm ready, Billy. I finished."

Billy turned and smiled, showing his back teeth and silver crown. He nodded and walked to the door.

"Meet me in the barn."

I ran to the back porch to get my denim jacket. It had been Billy's, was much too small for him now and still large on me though I was tall for eleven. Grandmother handed me my hat and gloves and grabbed tightly under my chin.

"Be careful with that ax, you. Wear your hat."

"It's a hatchet, grandma."

She kissed me on top of my head and I ran out the front door, around the roses, and across grandmother's truck garden toward the barn. Billy was just ahead wearing his denim jacket. He took long strides and made heel prints in the mud.

"Get the doors."

I watched him go in the double hung door at the side. I went to the front of the barn and tried to pull open the tall, wooden doors. The tractor started inside and Billy honked the horn. I pulled harder and harder and then Billy was above me opening the door while I struggled, dragging my feet in the mud. He got back on the tractor and I opened the other door for him and he drove through. I closed both doors and ran around and out the double-hung door.

Billy sat on the tractor levering the idle up and down and setting the lift. I climbed up to my usual place on his right and hooked my feet along the differential. Billy turned to me and took the hatchet and slipped it alongside the rope, come-along and double-bit in the dunnage box. We went past the house, the chicken shed filled with Grandma's ladies, and waited at the end of the drive. Billy gave me his frustrated look and put the tractor in neutral. I jumped down and opened the barbed wire gate. Billy drove through and I fastened the gate and had to run to catch up to the tractor and climb aboard.

We started down the hill and into the early morning fog. The sun was bright through partings in the heavy clouds and shined down to light the road in jagged patches. At the bottom of the hill the road went away and we were in open field, fallow and filled with sheep. We came to another gate. I jumped down before we got to it and ran ahead, opening and closing it as Billy drove through, catching up and expertly climbing onto the moving tractor.

When we got to the woods the road was still muddy from last night's thundershower. Water clung to the branches of the trees and rained down as we pushed our way through. It was dark and Billy turned on the tractor's single headlight. It bounced from tree to tree, flashing across the wet air in streaming bands. We came out of the woods and into another pasture. Cattle were bunched around a wire gate and Billy stopped the tractor and waited. He looked at me and then the cattle, their breath steaming in the early morning cold.

"That bull there's the one knocked me down last spring. He's one ornery bastard."

The bull looked at me and snorted into the ground. Billy looked at me and then at the bull and then back at me. I looked at the bull and then Billy and then at my boots on the differential. Billy shook his head, blew through his teeth and chuckled.

"I'll get the gate, pardoner. You pull her through."

The summer before Uncle Philip had showed me how to drive the tractor but I had never driven it alone. Billy opened the gate and I went through, jerking the tractor with the clutch and killing the engine when I stopped. Billy closed the gate and jumped up on the fender.

"Here. Let me take her."

I watched Billy for some sign of forgiveness but he stared forward into the fog and motioned with a nod of his head.

"We're going to that creek."

Just ahead was a cut along the road and a drop beyond.

"*The bull scared me, Billy.*"

"Hold on."

He pushed the throttle forward and the tractor launched itself in the mud. It sloughed from side to side along the bank of the creek. We stopped at the top and I saw into the bottom where it lay on its back, the eyes distended, the stomach bloated and skin taut across the belly. The legs locked outward and pointed to the sky.

"We want the calf. Probably we'll have to pull her out. We can use the tractor and the fence."

I looked at Billy. He didn't move at first, put the tractor in neutral and cocked his jaw in my direction.

"*Billy, I can drive.*"

He exhaled loudly through his teeth at the sky.

"Can you move her in line with the fence?"

"I can drive, Billy."

"Okay, line her up. We'll pull her out here, first."

Billy got the double-bit, come-along and a length of rope. I put the tractor into position and he fastened the rope around the cows' neck and to the fence. He motioned me to pull ahead and I did, stretching the rope until the cow popped free. I dragged it up the embankment, shut off the engine and joined Billy at the carcass. It had flies in its eyes and mouth. The nostrils were vacant, elongated holes and I could see deep inside them into the nasal cavity.

"She hasn't started to stink yet. I want to get her out before it gets warm."

I took the rope to the fence post and tied it with two half hitches and a granny. Billy tied the other end around the calf's head. He put the come-along back in the dunnage box and motioned me away.

"You watch that fence post."

Billy started the tractor and eased forward. The rope got tighter and tighter, aligning the carcass and calf with the fence. The fence post started bending and I ran to it, climbing through the wire and catching hold on the opposite side with my weight swinging backwards. I leaned backwards and dug in my boots and held until my purchase gave in the soft earth. I hollered at Billy and he looked at me just as the fence post buckled and cracked at the base. He stopped the tractor and came over, kicking at the bloated carcass as he passed. I looked away and then stared at my boots covered with mud.

"Goddamn it."

He turned, put his hands on his hips and stared hard at the fence post and then at me.

"Shit. Now I got to fix the goddamn fence."

Billy climbed back on the tractor and backed it, relieving the tension on the rope. I held the fence post while Billy wrapped it with wire. I untied the rope, Billy skeined it, looped one stiff leg jutting skyward and used the end to turn a bight.

"We'll drag her to the woods so we can use a tree. She's starting to stink already."

I collected the fence pliers and extra wire and took my place on the fender. I watched the carcass dragging behind as it caught and bucked on the ruts in the road. It rolled from side to side, got stuck in a furrow and Billy moved the throttle lever and shifted to low range to free it. I could hear the skeleton snacking. The neck hung loose-jointed and slack and the body rolled independent of the head. It made me feel sick to my stomach. I stared straight ahead but I could still hear the sound of the snacking.

The old bull watched us approach the gate. His eyes were bleary and sad as if he recognized the cow. He snorted at the ground and Billy stopped the tractor.

"Billy, He's one ornery bastard."

Billy looked straight ahead and then at me. He blew air through his teeth, slapped his hands on the steering wheel and climbed down from the tractor. I jumped down off the fender and ran past him.

"I'll get it."

He stopped and narrowed his eyes, shook his head and walked back to the tractor. I ran to the gate, opened it and stood close to the post while I kept my eye on the bull. Billy was almost through the gate when he charged. I thought that he was after me and I behind the fencepost but he went right for the tractor. I yelled at Billy who turned, saw the bull charging and blew the horn. The bull continued on-course and butted the side, ringing the fender where I usually sat and staggered off snorting white vapor into the cold air. Billy blew the horn again and the bull looked at me with its bleary and sad eyes, back at Billy and turned and walked away. I kept the post between me and the bull and as soon as Billy had pulled past I swung the gate closed and put the chain across the top. I ran to the tractor and climbed to the spot on Billy's right. Billy grinned at me and showed back teeth.

"He's one ornery bastard, Billy."

"Yup. That he is, pardoner."

Back on the fender I could see that the cow was trailing blood and skin was coming off its back in furry tufts. When Billy slowed for the woods the smell caught up to us. I had to hold my nose and breathe through my teeth. Billy pulled a bandanna from his jacket and tied it around his neck. He put it over his mouth and nose and motioned for me to do the same. The ground was dry out in the open where the sun was burning off the fog but in the woods it was still muddy. We dragged the carcass to the top of a crest and stopped at a wide, sun-lighted knoll in the fog. The rays came through the trees diffused and slanting and hung in the moisture. The trees looked like columns supporting a ceiling of fog at the top. A thick beam lit the carcass. We worked silently. I could hear the tink-tink of the engine as it cooled and smell the carcass among the dank foliage. Billy positioned the hindquarters across a bole and brought me the hatchet.

"Now real careful, while I pull. Go on, careful there," he whispered, pointing to the flesh constricting the calf.

I did as he instructed, hacking tentatively and trying not to hurt the calf. Billy pulled and grunted and nodded for me to continue. All at once the cow shuddered and a flood of offal, blood and placenta spilled onto my boots. Billy fell over backwards in the mud, the calf held high in one hand, free of the ground. He gained his feet and smiled so that his silver crown sparkled.

"Look here. She's perfect, just perfect. I ought to get half a grade for this."

The calf looked deformed. Veins protruded beneath the translucent skin. From the neck down it was emaciated and bone thin. The head was tumid by comparison, the eyes distorted and huge. The stench surrounded us and I gagged. Billy pulled his bandanna over his mouth and nose, cut the umbilical cord and wiped his hands on his jeans. The cow lay staring upward, its head canted away from its neck, its eyes imploring, the nasal cavity empty of flies. I turned away and Billy came around and held the calf in fron of him. I wiped at my eyes.

"Good work. We got her, pardoner."

He chucked me on the shoulder and I pushed his hand away. He took a piece of cord from his jacket pocket, bound the hind legs and suspended the miniature body from the lift.

"Let's go get some dinner," he said. "I could eat a cow."

On the ride back I stared straight ahead into the sun until it hurt my eyes. I opened all the gates and climbed back aboard each time, but I sat forward on the fender and did not look at Billy. At the house, I put his old denim jacket under the shoe mantle in the gallery off the kitchen and went upstairs to my room. At supper I sat in my usual place on Billy's right but I couldn't look at him. He tried to make funny jokes but what he said didn't seem so special anymore.

I spent the next day helping grandmother in the garden, feeding her ladies, collecting their eggs and filling the wood box on the porch. Michael went out the next day with Billy and I left the following morning.

It has been fifteen years since Uncle Philip died and now Billy runs the farm with help from men he hires in town. I live half a continent away, far removed from the country summers of my youth. Sometimes, at odd moments, I think about the farm, that morning in the fog, and Billy. I imagine his old denim jacket is still beneath the shoe mantle. I doubt that he remembers me.

Red Tail of Contrition

Our bird won't eat. Feathers are dull and matted.
Alert almond eyes murky and yellow like an old convertible
car with a weathered, rear window. Sometimes you see
people who have cut rectangles in the windows or put slits
wide enough to see but still keep the heat inside. My sister
has a Fiat with a yellowed, rear window. It turns the world to
just shapes and shadows, indistinctly familiar forms and
movements. I wouldn't want our bird to see like that. She
deserves better.

Rick says we never should have put the sock over
her head. That kills the olfactory, blurs the predatory scent,
short circuits the raptor's world view. Anthony argues she's
too young, nothing more, nothing less. I'm new to falconry
and haven't an opinion, but I know when a thing isn't right.

It began with snakes. Rick and Anthony came by on their bicycles and pounded on my bedroom window. Rick shined his flashlight into my eyes to see if I were awake. He had his army surplus backpack, a snake stick with a heavy wire loop and coils of rope criss-crossed on his pack. Anthony had a shovel tied to his handlebars. We rode through the quiet morning streets, stopping to check residential trash cans for salvageable treasure, and hid our bicycles in a ditch of Manzanita and Toyon along the chain link fence that separates our community from Standard Oil property. Rick climbed over and Anthony tossed the backpack, the snake stick and then the shovel. I had my Scout knife my grandmother sent me last year for my thirteenth birthday.

The oil fields are just outside the town limits. We've been here many times. One night, when Rick had swiped a bottle of Schnapps from his father, we rode the pumpers. It was a little tricky at first. I wasn't clear as to how you mounted the rotating flywheel. Rick went first and with dumb trust I imitated his moves. It turned out all right, but I don't think I'll do it again. You really could get hurt, I suppose, if things were to go differently.

Rick is hard-core. He was elected as half a delegation to represent our scout troop at the annual scout jamboree. He never misses an outing, even though he has no father, and spends a lot of time reading about warfare and survival. I think that I am going but I'll be more like support crew. Our troop can only afford to send one scout. Of course it's Rick as the one but my mother said she'd pay half my way if I promise to do my schoolwork and help her out more. I figure that I can get my dad to chip in the rest. I'll ask him when I see him next weekend. First, he'll talk about responsibility and the value of a dollar. Mostly he'll feel guilty for leaving us and shacking up with Sharon. Then he'll give in. Usually, if I work it right, he gives me what I want.

The jamboree is mostly a bunch of tests about scouting, environment, knots and general woodsmanship. Rick's a Life Scout and I just made Star, though actually I've already earned two extra merit badges on my way to Life. I think I can make it before the jamboree if I take swimming lessons this summer.

What Rick wants is a skin for his hat. He got the idea from reading a book about infantry in Australia, and he thinks that if we are to make a lasting impression on the other troops, we need hats with snakeskin hatbands. Specifically, we need bush hats, with one side pinned upwards with snake skins sewn to the crown. Of course to be authentic, the skins should be copperhead or sidewinder. Those aren't in our area, so instead he decided the skin of the feared western diamondback would have to do. With this in mind, he made the snake loop. I'm not certain what the shovel is for.

Just inside the chain link fence there's a storm drain that goes to the main boulevard. If discovered, this is our escape route. Rick shows us how to get around the grating, and draws a map in the dirt to explain the course of the pipe. If all else fails, he says, we can dive into the storm drain, make our way to the boulevard and emerge ahead of any pursuers. With a little luck, they won't get a clean shot. Rick reminds us that we are trespassing on the property of an influential, multinational corporation. I listen and look at Anthony. He turns away and puts his beret inside his fatigue jacket. The stuff about shooting seems unlikely, but Rick can be dramatic and it makes our quest seem more dangerous. I look at the map and think about the length of the pipe and all the rats that live there. I heard a story about people flushing alligators down toilets and how they live in the sewers beneath the streets. I don't trust the pipe. If worse comes to worse, I think I'll go easy, surrender with my hands in the air, give in and face the consequences. My dad says you always have to face the consequences. I think that I could get out of it with just grounding or some extra chores or something. It wouldn't be too bad. I could get my little brother to help. Rick smoothes dirt on the map and then stomps on top to erase all evidence. Take no chances, he says, and starts up the road along the fence.

We hike for a half an hour and stop to rest. Rick explains about rattlers, where to look and how to recognize them. Make a lot of noise he says, if you don't want to accidently step on one, but if you want to catch one, and we do, walk lightly and look for anything like a stick lying in the sunshine. They come out in the morning to warm up, so they can hunt. That's why the best time to catch them is early, better yet if it's a bit cold. They don't move so well in cold weather. They like to go slowly into the day, sunbathe first, then, when their blood is good and warm and all is right, they go looking for food. Not always, of course. Sometimes they just lie around and digest the stuff they ate yesterday or the day before. We'll probably find them near the water, or right at the edge of a clearing. You can mistake them for a stick, so don't try to pick up any sticks, he says. Then he breaks off a sapling and takes a hatchet from his pack and blunts both ends. He gives it to me. Just poke first, he says, before you step. Remember, a rattlesnake is more afraid of you than you are of it, he says, pointing his finger for effect. Then he points at the sapling and makes a poking motion with his arms. Oh, he adds; a rattlesnake bite will kill you.

In my rush this morning I forgot to eat any breakfast. Now not only am I hungry but I need to go to the bathroom. Rick produces a ziplock plastic bag of blue flowered toilet paper, in folded sheets, hands me the shovel and tells me to be expeditious. He's always using big words like expeditious or calamity or discombobulated. He's two years older than I am, but only one year ahead of me in school. He was kept back a year and so he thinks he's smarter than everyone else. He's pretty tall, too: but I know more than he does about almost everything except snakes.

Watch where you step, he says, as I climb down the embankment. It's tough, walking through the bramble bush and watching for snakes at the same time. I pick my way carefully, find a suitable spot, get on with my business in a hurried way and return, running the last few steps trying not to think about where I'm stepping. Rick and Anthony have stripped to dark t-shirts. Anthony has a headband on and when I hand him the shovel, he stands with it poised at attention. Rick checks the toilet paper, looks at the number of sheets, seals them in the plastic bag and puts them in his pack. He leads us along the fence and then down, climbing and sliding, into the ravine.

Rick and Anthony walk quietly, watchful and aware. Rick pokes at fallen sticks and loose brush with the snake snare. Anthony swings the shovel to the side of him, scraping the ground three feet from where he steps. First he scraps one side then the other. I'm careful and step directly in the spots where they've already stepped. I probe with my fresh sapling but without much enthusiasm. Rick turns and directs me to the right, out of their trail. Anthony moves to the left, and between us we cover an area about fifteen feet wide. We get to the bottom of the ravine and stop at a rotting log to rest. Anthony takes off his headband, which is actually a washed out kerchief, and wipes his forehead. Rick kneels on one knee and studies the ground. He puts his cheek down in the dirt, than licks his finger and first holds it up in the air and then down on the ground. Warming up, he says, and Anthony nods with approval.

"Should see some a . . . a . . . action soon."

Anthony doesn't say much. He stutters really badly in school. He doesn't stutter much around me, but I guess he got into the habit of not speaking from being around other people. I have a speech impediment myself. I can't say esses. Words like snow or snake just don't want to come out. Anthony and I go to speech therapy together Monday and Wednesday. The therapist gives me drills that I practice while walking to school and workbook exercises that I have to do out loud at night. I'm getting better. My sister still teases me, though. She's a real pain in the ass.

I ask Rick what we'll do if one of us gets bit. Anthony looks sideways at me, spits, and says `suck it out' like he's done it a million times. Rick removes a flat, gray rubber ball from his pack. He separates it into two parts, shows me the scalpel, smelling ammonia and instruction booklet. He demonstrates the suction of one of the rubber balls on my arm. It works pretty well and leaves a red welt. I study the booklet. It says that the key is not to panic, to lie down comfortably and try to slow your heartbeat. Then make two incisions over the fang holes and use the rubber ball to draw out the venom. In exceptional circumstances, of multiple strikes, apply a tourniquet between the puncture and the heart and immediately seek medical attention. At the bottom there's a note that says sometimes the snake refuses to release it's grip and must be forcibly removed. I don't know how you could do that. I ask Rick and he just shrugs his shoulders, holds up the hatchet and puts the booklet, smelling ammonia and scalpel in the rubber balls. Anthony spits and says he was almost bit once. It happened when he was at summer camp, hunting for arrowheads in some rocks. He reached for a rock and heard the rattle of a ferocious five footer. He couldn't find anything to smack it so he tried to hit it with the rock. His throw went wide and the snake retreated beneath a boulder. Anthony came back later, with a shovel and a broom, and tried to force the snake out. It didn't work and he says he'll get that snake next time his parents let him go to summer camp. It sounds like a lot of big talk but Anthony's done some pretty wild things before so I imagine most of what he says is true. He's going to military school next year, if his parents can afford it, and learn to fly jets in the Air Force. Everyone knows his parents haven't much money. They live below the boulevard in the houses that back up against the railroad tracks. I don't want to tell him that, because who knows, maybe he'll make it. It's hard to say what some guys will do if they want something bad enough.

We're walking in single file along the bottom of the dry ravine. Here and there we have to force our way through bramble brush or go around a copse of scrub oak. We walk for about fifteen minutes, in silence, Rick leading the way and then stop at a cane break about ten feet high. Anthony takes the hatchet from Rick's pack. wedges his way into the cane and emerges with a tall, budded stalk. He sections it into three-foot lengths, wraps them together with his headband and puts them in Rick's backpack. He looks at Rick and they both smile, like I don't know anything about drugs, and we start walking. I know about them, but that doesn't mean I smoke them. The ravine flattens some, widens almost to the width of a street, and the undergrowth thins. There are fallen trees along the shoulders and ahead a tree connects the banks of the ravine. Rick holds up his hand and stops. He slowly removes the backpack, sets it down, and shapes a loop in the end of the snare. Anthony stands poised with his shovel. I'm looking around the ground ahead but I see nothing. Rick looks at me and then points to the fallen tree. There, draped across the end, its head on the ground on one side and its tail on the ground on the other, is the snake. It looks very peaceful, its scaly skin shining in the sunshine, its tongue licking in and out from the triangular head. I can see the eyes, hooded and dark, and the slow movement of the breathing.

"Diamondback," Rick says; "the fiercest of the western rattlers."

He crouches down and begins to approach.

"Stay behind the sun," he whispers, and Anthony bends low and moves the opposite direction. I drop to one knee and wait. The snake's tongue continues to dart in and out of its mouth. A ripple goes through his body, across the part on the tree and stops at the rattles. He doesn't move, but as Rick and Anthony approach he lifts his head and looks toward me. Rick says snakes use mostly smell and don't see very well. I know what that's like because last year when I hit only .137 but stole a lot of bases, my dad took me to the optometrist and told him I couldn't see the ball. Now I have to wear glasses all the time. I can see real well with them but guys at school started to call me four eyes. Most of them are bigger than I am so what can I do? My mom says it's okay, just do well in your classes and you'll show them when report cards come out. That sounds great to her but she doesn't get the treatment all the time like I do. My sister doesn't have to wear glasses, either, or my mom or dad. So far it's just me born with crummy eyes. I hope my little brother doesn't have to go through the same thing. It really stinks.

Rick has the loop in front of him. All of a sudden the snake starts moving. I'm not certain at first, but the diamonds shift and ripple and now I can see that one after another is disappearing over the edge of the tree. Anthony is on the other side and has the shovel out. He stabs at the snake and it disappears beneath the brush. Anthony is right after it and Rick goes around the other side of the brush and tells Anthony to flush it out. Then there is a scurrying and a ringing and the rattle like something dry or broken in the wind.

"He struck th . . . th . . . th . . . shovel."

I see him stabbing into the brush with the blade and then he motions me to join him. The snake is coiled now, the head bobbing back and forth, watching the shovel blade. Rick reaches in through the brush and drops the loop over the tail. He yells and drags the snake out into the open. Anthony and I run around and there he is, a fat, four footer. Anthony snacks at the head and manages to pin it down. Rick takes my sapling and wedges it on the back of the neck and Anthony takes the shovel blade, places it alongside the sapling and gives it a good shove with his foot. The body is thrashing around, whipping the snare around on the ground. Rick gets on the shovel and jumps down with all his weight and the head shoots off a few feet toward me. I jump backwards and suddenly feel sick. The jaws are clamping open and closed and venom is squirting out around the fangs. Rick cheers and Anthony pushes me aside and smacks the head with the shovel. One of the eyes is hanging out, attached with a string and the jaws continue to open and close. Rick takes the shovel and digs a hole and pushes the head into it. He tells me to find some rocks and put them on top of the head. Then he covers it with dirt and goes back to get the body. It is just barely moving now, the glistening diamonds dull and the rattles flattened where Anthony hit them. Rick takes a plastic baggie from the pack and puts the body in it. He hands it around to feel. It is still moving some and I feel the warmth through the baggie. I feel the muscle as it writhes. The scales have scraped off in some places and blood oozes from the cut opening. The color is duller, even when Rick holds it up to the sun, the rattles are smashed to bits, the body crudely hacked and scarred in places. It looks dull and lifeless. I feel sick and a little hungry at the same time.

"W . . . w . . . we . . . d . . . did it," Anthony says. He takes the baggie from Rick and holds it over his head like Conan the Barbarian or something. Rick scrapes off the shovel blade in the dirt and collects the backpack and snake loop. He takes out a pack of cigarettes and he and Anthony light them up like they're really smoking.

"That's one for me, guys, now let's get us some more," Rick says. "Come on."

We start walking, spreading out the same way and watching the ground. Rick points to a nest in a tree on the other side of the bank ahead. We all stop to look up and then a bird takes off from the nest. We watch the flight. He doesn't look too stable. He flies like one of those goony birds they show on National Geographic. The bird isn't really flapping its wings very well. It sort of falls at an angle and then it crashes into a bush. Rick starts running and Anthony and I follow. Rick scrambles into the bush while I stand outside watching the bird struggle, falling deeper and deeper as it does, into the branches. It cries out and you see now that it's a young hawk. Rick and Anthony work around to each side of it. Anthony reaches for it and it cries again. Rick grabs it from the other side and it stops crying. He wraps his hand around the body, holding the wings close to its sides and climbs out from the bush. It is dark red, less than a foot tall and it has the clearest eyes that I've ever seen. It looks right at me and I can tell its frightened.

"J . . . J . . . J . . . Jesus, man. It's a red-tail hawk," Anthony says. "We ca . . . ca . . . ca . . . caught a red tail hawk."

Rick holds it up next to his chest and puts his other hand around it.

"She's beautiful," he says. "I always wanted a hawk."

We all stare at the bird. It turns its head, watching the three of us, from side to side. Rick strokes it with the thumb of one hand. He hands it to Anthony and sits down on the ground.

"We'll have to get it out of here before the mother returns. She'll attack us."

He removes his shoe and takes off a sock. He takes the bird from Anthony and instructs him to put the sock over the head.

"Watch for the mother," he says to me.

I look upward and see nothing but the sky. All around it is light and hot. No wind moves.

"Why d . . . do you get it ?" Anthony says.

Rick gets the sock securely down over the body and holds the bird out for me to feel.

"I have the most training and I can take care of it. I know more about hawks and snakes than you do," he says.

The bird is very still in my hands. The racing beat of the heart can be felt through the sock, and now and then it shudders, twists its neck and makes a sound. I hand it back to Rick.

"Maybe we should let it go," I say. "It's wild. It doesn't belong to us."

Rick turns on me quickly, looks me down and picks up the backpack and snake loop. He begins walking ahead and Anthony and I look at each other while he keeps going.

"It sh . . . ou . . . ou . . . ld be mine," he says.

Rick stops and looks back to us. Then he walks off. Anthony picks up his shovel and we follow. No one says anything, even after we catch up with Rick, until we get to the fence. I climb over and Anthony throws the shovel, snake loop and backpack to me. He climbs up and straddles the fence. Rick hands him the hawk and he hands it to me. It is shaking and the claws are curled up. Then the snake is tossed over to Anthony. Rick joins us and puts the red tail in his shirt and we get our bikes and ride back. At my house, Rick rides past without saying anything. Anthony stops and gives me the snake.

"You'll h . . . have to skin him," he says. I look at the baggie, now partially filled with yellowish fluid, the colors on the skin completely gone and shake my head. Anthony gets on his bike and rides after Rick, the snake swinging from his handlebars as he peddles. Inside the house my mother asks me where I've been and I tell her about the hawk but not about the snake. First she gets sort of mad at me for trespassing and then really mad at me for taking the hawk from its natural habitat. I say that we're going to take care of it and teach it to fly. She shakes her head at me and asks me how I'd feel if I were the red tail taken from my mother. I go downstairs to my room in the basement. It is cool here beneath ground level. On the wall there is a map of the world, my Le Mans poster of Steve McQueen, and a chart of the solar system. I lie down on my little brother's bed. I don't feel tired but I feel bad. I feel a little bad about the snake but really bad about the red tail. It's not something an almost Life Scout going to a jamboree would do. My little brother comes downstairs and asks me to help him ride his bike. We go out front and I hold the seat while he pedals around the driveway. He is shaky and goes too slowly to stay upright. He needs my help to start and stop and I have to grab him sometimes when he forgets to pedal. Sometimes he just stops and almost falls into the station wagon. I have to teach him because he's young. We practice until he gets tired and he goes inside for a drink, but I can't stop thinking about the red tail. I get on my bike and ride out the driveway. I know what I need to do. Rick's house is only a couple of miles away.

Painting with Jeremiah

They stood alongside a decrepit and rust-mottled panel van. Craggy, rust oxide fingers reached upward from the rocker panels in confederation with water and time; bubbling holes spread like cancer from bumper to bumper. Not one wheel boasted a hubcap yet the tires were new and the van clean. A clever, black iron roof rack with fleur de lis at each corner held aluminum extension ladders. Open cargo doors exposed a complex array of rollers and paintbrushes that swung in some otherworldly meter with the gusting wind, clattering against a metal rack filled with paint buckets, hand tools, old coffee cans of hardware and canvas drop cloths. The tall, teenage boy kicked at the rusted rocker, dislodging a chunk of metal that fell to the ground.

"'Get you 'new rig, man. Motherfucker's rusted ta shit."

The old man squatted in the gravel against the windward side of the van. He wore an Angels' baseball cap, paint splattered canvas overalls, and a creased, long sleeved, white shirt.

"Rust does what rust does. That is its nature."

The wind gusted and rattled the paint rollers. A multi-colored advertisement skidded across the drive and lodged against a front wheel. The tall, teenage boy kicked it free with a pair of unlaced, basketball sneakers.

"Looka this shit."

The old man kneeled over a pail of thinner. He dipped a brush, held it above the pail, and watched the liquid drip. With thick, paint-stained fingers he massaged the bristles from band to tip, each time squeezing thinner and paint into the pail and flicking tiny droplets from his neatly trimmed nails. He lifted the brush to peer through it as beads of thinner slid down the handle into the pail.

"Shit...."

The procedure was repeated, without haste, while the tall teenager chopped with his brush at the ground and tossed it into a battered, wooden box. Every few minutes the old man lifted another of the cleaned brushes above his head, rotated it in the fading sunlight and peered through the gleaming bristles toward the rain clouds ganging overhead.

He took a clean rag from his overalls and began wiping the brush, working from the handle, corralling sections of bristles like handfuls of damp hair and drying them with the rag. After he finished, he held the brush close to his weathered face, closed his black eyes and passed the bristles beneath a red, gin-blossomed nose. He wrapped the brush in a folded sheet of newspaper, placed it into the wooden box and picked up another.

"Motherfucker, why you take so much time wi' that shit? Get the hell outta here."

The old man continued dipping and caressing the paint from the brush into the pail.

"We do everything the same. Good painting; good cleaning. It is all the same."

"I ain't no painter, man. Jus' took the job for the fuckin' money."

"Everything is the same. Paint good; clean good."

"Shit. I play ball, that's what I do good."

"There is no difference."

"Well 'No Difference,' get up there and collect the check. I wanta get the fuck goin'."

"We go when the job is done, Jeremiah. And not before."

Jeremiah walked to the passenger side of the van and returned with a hooded windbreaker. He thrust his hands through the armholes, jerked it over his head and scratched at a mess of dark, matted hair. He dug in his jeans pocket, pulled out a book of matches and shook the last cigarette from a pack. He jammed the cigarette past a permanent scowl, crumpled the empty package and threw it at the ground. It caught the wind before touching down, skidded across the drive and lodged against a stone border. He snapped the matches against the book and tried to hide the flame in cupped hands. Again and again he tried, each time cursing and tossing the spent match onto the ground; and each time it smoldered in the wind and was swept across the curved driveway to the road. Finally, a cloud of blue smoke rose from his hands and he leaned back and exhaled at the sky. The old man was staring across the half-circle drive.

"Mothafuckin' wind."

Jeremiah slouched against the van and kicked again at the jagged hole.

"I drop this cig into that thinner and we'd have some kinda party. Shit would go sky high, huh?"

The old man looked up, his face calm and inscrutable, a rag wiping the last brush in his hands. He squinted with one eye and struggled to rise.

"Don't fool with thinner, Jeremiah. It is not like us. Thinner cannot change its nature."

"Motherfucka, just get with it and le's go."

The old man gained his feet, massaged his left leg and wiped his hands on the rag.

"All right. Put away the thinner. I will talk to Mrs. Robinson."

"Fuckin' right you will."

The old man went to the driver's door of the van, retrieved a clipboard and passed his hand through his short, clipped hair. He arched his back, smoothed the front of his shirt and straightened his cap. He pulled on a blue, paint-splattered nylon jacket, looked up at Jeremiah, smoking where he leaned against the van, and smiled. Jeremiah tilted back his head, narrowed his green eyes and glowered through the haze.

"I will be a few minutes. Smoke another cigarette, why don't you?"

Jeremiah waved him off, muttering, and sat down on the threshold of the van's open doors. He pulled the hood of his windbreaker over his head so that only nose, mouth and stubbled chin were visible. One hand passed in and out of the hood while he kept the other fisted deep in the pocket of his baggy jeans. Above him, thunderheads gathered in the dark sky. Bronzed lights shaped like Pagodas lit the half-circle drive and a flood light at the base of a towering pine next to the house flickered off and on. Jeremiah watched the old man at the front porch talking to a slender, blond woman holding a little girl in her arms. They stood on the porch, the old man drawing with his finger on the clipboard, both of their heads nodding up and down. The little girl squirmed in her mother's arms and she set her down. She looked at Jeremiah, put her hands to her mouth and stuck out her tongue. Then she giggled, jumped in place and ran into the house slamming the door behind her. The old man and the woman stepped off the porch, looked up and stared together at the sky.

"No shit, lady, its a motherfuckin' storm."

Jeremiah spat his cigarette butt onto the ground. The tip flared when it struck and was carried off in the wind. The woman talked with the old man, looked toward Jeremiah, waved and smiled. She stroked her shoulder length hair and tucked it behind her ears. Jeremiah peered from beneath the hooded windbreaker and nodded his head.

"I'd do that bitch."

The woman and the old man disappeared around the side of the house. Jeremiah looked at the sky and dug both hands into the pockets of his jeans. The woman and the old man reappeared, heads raised, pointing at the clouds above them.

"Come the fuck on, old man. What the motherfuckin' problem?"

The old man was pointing to the clipboard. He removed papers, gave them to the woman and she folded them as she stepped onto the porch. She went inside the house for a few seconds and then returned with a checkbook.

"Fuck yea, we're gettin' somewhere."

Jeremiah tore open a new pack of cigarettes and leaned into the van. He struck at a match and the tip of the cigarette flared. In front of the porch, the old man tilted back his head and then spread both arms to his sides catching raindrops in his upturned hands. The woman tore the check from her checkbook, handed it to the old man and disappeared into the house. The old man folded the check, put it in his pocket and limped across the yard.

"Le's go. Get the fuck outa here."

The old man looked up at him, his head concealed beneath the hood of the windbreaker, cigarette smoke like a gray mask floating over his face.

"Just one thing to do. That is all."

"Fuck that! We did our part."

The old man went to the van and began to gather tools from the back.

"What the fuck? What're you doin'?"

"The bedroom shutter is loose. It was not tightened when it was painted."

"Hey, let the fuckin' handyman do it. We're painters."

"It needs to be tightened. We do it."

"Motherfucka. The rich bitch is trying to get something outa you for free. Tell her ta hire a fuckin' handyman."

The old man turned in his tracks, fixed his eyes on Jeremiah and stepped close. He looked up into his face, inches away and raised a pointed finger. Rainwater bounced off his cap, his forehead and dripped from his nose. He spoke just above a whisper.

"The *ladder man* should have tightened it."

Jeremiah flicked his cigarette to the ground, mashed it into the gravel drive and dropped his head. The old man held his position, staring into Jeremiah's face, and then turned away and unfastened an extension ladder from the roof of the van. He reached it to his shoulder, hooked one arm through a rung and balanced it in place. Jeremiah kicked at the gravel drive and climbed into the van. The old man moved slowly across the yard, favoring one leg, with the extension ladder on his shoulder. Jeremiah sat with his knees against his chest and sneakers propped on the dashboard watching the raindrops splatter off the windshield.

"Motherfucka'. *The ladder man.*"

Jeremiah watched the old man round the corner of the house, climbed out of the van and slammed the door. He shoved his hands into the pockets of his windbreaker and started across the yard. In the front window of the house, the little girl stood with a toy at her mouth. Jeremiah looked up and she stuck out her tongue. He stopped in surprise, his eyes wide with a thin smile wrinkling his lip. The little girl laughed, jumped up and down, and waved. Jeremiah smiled, pulled one hand free, wiggled his fingers, and then looked around in a panic. He shoved his hand back into his windbreaker, pulled the hood close against the rain and walked around the corner.

The old man had the extension ladder near the pine tree and extended to a second story gable. Jeremiah stepped up beside him and grabbed hold of a rung.

"I'm the *ladder man*, right? That's why you fuckin' hired me, right, old man?"

The old man paused, and then pointed to the gable and held out a screwdriver.

"Shit, man. I know which fuckin' one."

Jeremiah took the screwdriver and started climbing the extension ladder. He stopped at the second rung and looked down.

"After this, we fuckin' done, right? No more handyman shit?"

"Then the job will be done."

"Motherfuckin' right it done."

The wind gusted through the rungs of the extension ladder and rain fell harder and pelted the window glass of the gable. Carriage lamps flanking a bench on the back porch lit just as a flash of lightning and thunder filled the sky. Jeremiah climbed the extension ladder, stabbing at each rung with his unlaced sneakers, shaking the ladder with each step. The old man stood beneath him steadying the rails with both arms. At the top, Jeremiah reached across and examined the latch. It was hanging from the siding by one screw. He held it in place and tightened the loose screw. It turned and turned.

"Shit!"

He stopped, looked at the old man, the shutter and then the old man again. Another flash of lightning lit the sky and thunder cracked above the house. Jeremiah balanced on the extension ladder and looked in the window. He watched as the woman passed in the second story hallway followed by the little girl. The rain began to fall sideways, blowing in Jeremiah's face, pouring off the roof and splashing on the ground. Jeremiah climbed down, water dripping from the hood of his windbreaker and stood facing the old man.

"It's fucked up, man. I can't fix it. And it's raining fuckin' bad."

The wind gusted as if in answer and the shutter swung and smacked against the gable. The latch dropped to the ground at their feet.

"Fuck it. Fuck it! We 'spose ta be painting the trim not fixing it. Tell that rich bitch ta get a handyman."

The old man stooped and picked up the latch. The screw was still attached and he examined it as his palms filled with water and rain dripped off his cap.

"It needs longer screws. That is all. I have a can in the rack."

"Oh shit. Man, It's fuckin' raining. Let's get the fuck outta here."

The old man started toward the van but Jeremiah cut him off.

"This is bullshit. That's lightnin' there. You ain't s'pose to be out in fuckin' lightnin'."

The old man fixed his hard stare on Jeremiah and held the latch up in his hand.

"Needs longer screws."

"Shit! You like lightnin' or somethin'?"

"Lightning is lightning. It does not know how to be anything other than its nature. Go sit in the van if you are afraid. Sit and smoke your cigarette."

The old man waved his arm at the dark sky and wiped the water from his weathered face. Jeremiah slapped at his thighs, his eyes bright, a red flush beneath the hood glowing across his forehead.

"Motherfucka. I ain't 'fraid a nothin'."

He stomped past the old man toward the van. The shutter banged again with a gust of wind and the woman appeared in the window. She waved at the old man standing in the rain, crossed her arms over her chest and shuddered as if cold. Jeremiah returned with the coffee can of screws, and the old man sorted through them. Another flash of lightning lit the sky, followed by a rolling crash of thunder. Jeremiah jumped in place and then wiped his face with his hand. He looked up at the sky as the old man put two long screws in his hand. Jeremiah shook his head and muttered as walked to the extension ladder.

"Fuckin' bullshit, man. That's lightnin'."

He held onto a rung and looked at the sky.

"Motherfuckin' whacked."

He put one foot on the first rung, hesitated and looked at the dark sky.

"Sit in the truck ladder man if you are afraid. I will do it."

Jeremiah slapped at the extension ladder with one hand and pointed at the old man.

"I fuckin' told ya, I ain't 'fraid."

The old man shrugged his shoulders and stuck out his hand. He raised it palm up and smiled.

"Motherfucka' . . . . "

Jeremiah climbed the extension ladder and held the shutter flush to the side of the house. With the other hand he tightened each screw in the latch and then hooked the catch. Thunder boomed overhead and a lightning bolt exploded in the pine tree. Jeremiah saw the flash and then as if outside himself watched his body slide down the extension ladder. He descended in slow motion, hands loose but grasping the rails, passing one rung at a time and when he reached the ground he rolled onto his back. Everything was silent and then he saw himself, rain pelting his face and hands, while peering over him stood the old man and the woman. The old man helped him sit up. Jeremiah blinked his eyes several times and looked at himself sitting on the ground in the rainwater. Then he was back, shaking his head from side to side. He touched his face with both hands. His eyebrows were singed and curled, and the front of his dark hair was kinked and crisp. The old man helped him to his feet and led him to the bench on the porch. The woman wrapped a heavy blanket around his shoulders and rubbed his back.

"Wha' happened?"

"Lightning, Jeremiah. It struck the tree and charged the ladder, too. Are you all right?"

"Huh?"

"Are you hurt?"

"I don't think so."

The woman bent down beside him.

"Should I call emergency?"

The old man pushed back the hood and looked into his face. Jeremiah poked at his singed eyebrows and the front of his hair. Then he shoved the old man's hand, shook his head and tilted back his face with narrowed eyes.

"Let go of me. I don't need no help."

Jeremiah stood up and brushed the mud from his pants.

"Let's get goin'."

Jeremiah stood and crossed the yard. He climbed into the van, wedged his sneakers against the dashboard, lit a cigarette, and smoked as the old man retrieved the extension ladder and strapped it to the rack.

"Come on, le's go man …."

The rain pounded the roof, ringing the sheet metal like a steel drum. Jeremiah finished the cigarette and flipped it out the window. The old man stowed the tools in the back of the van, climbed into the driver's seat and started the motor.

"Are you sure you are all right?"

"Get goin', man."

The old man wiped at his face with a towel while the motor idled. He waited as the van warmed up, switched on the heater fan and looked over at the house. The woman was crossing the yard with a raincoat held over her head. In her other hand was a paper bag. She stopped at the passenger window and Jeremiah rolled it down.

"I thought some brownies might make you feel better. Caroline helped."

She smiled and passed the paper bag to Jeremiah.

"Uh, thanks."

She turned and ran back to the porch, stood and waved from the doorway. Jeremiah opened the bag and took out a brownie.

"Hey, they're warm."

"A nice lady, that Mrs. Robinson."

A smile tugged at the corners of Jeremiah's mouth as he bit into the brownie.

"Yea. Nice lady."

The old man's eyes twinkled as the brownie disappeared into the hood of the windbreaker. The van pulled around the half-circle drive and stopped at the shrubbery. Raindrops bounced off the windshield and puddled around the tires.

"Wha?"

The old man shook his head and opened the driver's door. Jeremiah watched him a few seconds, got out, went to the shrubbery and picked up the crumpled cigarette package and advertisment. He climbed in and slammed the door.

"All right already! Le's go, man. This job's done."

"That is right," the old man said. "This job is done."

About the author

John White was born in Seattle, Washington. He lives in Altadena, California, where he writes and teaches as an Adjunct Professor at a local community college. His memoir, "Dog Lessons," won an IPPY Silver Medal. His short stories have won an El Dorado Writer's Guild Award and the First Place Fiction Editor's Prize Contest of the Grasslands Review. His memoir "Dog Lessons," and the novels "Hard Reset" and "A Piece of the Rock" in the Martin Gardens series are available on Amazon.